The River Boy

❖❖❖❖❖❖❖❖❖❖❖❖❖

Jessica Brown

Finch & Fellow
PUBLISHING HOME

FOR SIMON

Contents

CONTENTS

The River Boy

Montana
1909

My River

My summer started so plain, I would have never guessed it was going to be so special.

It was the last day of school. We were cleaning up from our pageant the night before. Taking down banners. Folding away our colored streamers.

All around me, the other kids were making their summer plans. Jackson and Peter were going to try to climb Black Rock. Lucy and Meredith were going to make a whole new set of cornhusk dolls, with dresses in the newest fashion.

"Clara!" Lucy said. "You can come over to my house. It's not such a bad walk for you, from your place."

"My" place was Ransom Ranch. From the front gate, my family's ranch was two miles outside of our town. It ran for miles in the opposite way, back to the sloping hills at the foot of the mountains. Our land was mostly wide-open, flat pasture for cattle. But there were tall pines around our wooden farmhouse, and a small circle of green apple trees behind the barn. And all kinds of trees grew along the river—aspens, pines, birches, maples.

"You bet I can," I said. I was known for being frank and jolly, always up for a good game of Red Rover or tug-of-war. I didn't tell lies and didn't snitch. A friend to everyone, I was known as.

For a moment, I liked the idea of walking over to Lucy's and making dolls. But when I looked down at the dark green banner I was folding, the thought made me feel hollow.

Lucy and Meredith were so close, and they seemed to really like dolls. When I played with those girls, a part of me felt left out.

And I could have tagged along with Jackson and Peter, but I felt left out then too. I liked to watch for robin redbreasts and hunt for the violets and clover hiding in the shadows. With Jackson and Peter, I felt rushed along, or silly and slow for taking my time.

Pa sometimes said, "It's a lonely old world," and Ma would say back, "If it wasn't so interesting." I didn't know who was right.

From out of my school desk, I gathered my little stash of pretty finds. A gray-blue bird feather, pretty as a magician's cap. The hugest maple leaf I'd ever seen, all the way back from autumn. A piece of a robin's egg shell that looked like fancy china. A red clay stone I had found one day in my left boot. An antique hairpin from underneath the schoolhouse. And a dried bouquet of lemon verbena that kept my desk smelling fresh.

I carefully folded my handkerchief around a fancy card from my teacher. It said: "Patience Is a Virtue." She gave it to me when I was being too huffy with my spelling team. I slipped the little wooden whistle my brother Caleb made for my birthday into my dress pocket. I retied the blue ribbon around my flyaway, strawberry-blonde hair. I was ready to head home.

I walked with Meredith, Lucy, Jackson, and Peter for the first half mile. We were all glad that Lucy's older brothers, Presley and Wyatt, hadn't come to school that day—they were mean bullies. So we walked free and easy through our little town, by the post office and the grocer's, and Miss Tilly's ice cream parlor. There was a stately church and two taverns, all their doors closed. It wasn't too busy this time of day. It was like the town was getting ready for summer too.

Then came the corner where I always turned and they always kept walking. I said my goodbyes and turned down the small road.

I stood under a small round of birches and waited. Soon, Little Jimmy turned the corner too, waving goodbye to his pack of young friends. He was a sweet boy, only five years old. I gave him a clove candy I had been saving for him, and we walked the next stretch together.

Soon, Little Jimmy turned in at his family's farm, and I waved goodbye to him too. Then it was just me and the road and the oaks lining the road and the long meadows behind the oaks. The big summer sky was overhead, lacy clouds to the north, right above the mountains.

I tried to look for birds. Or sweet clover for sachets. Or strange-shaped leaves to dry and display. But that hollow feeling inside me was too strong to let me see much.

The house was quiet when I arrived. Ma was out with Pa, weeding the cornfield a few acres north. My older brothers, Caleb and Jake, were still on their way back from Swan River Ranch, where they had been making trades that day.

I tucked away my school collection with my home collection and put the Patience card on my dresser. Then I changed my school clothes for chore clothes, a dusty pair of overalls. Time to round up the hens and bring the milk cows home and give the pig his slop. I whistled "Shine On, Harvest Moon" while I worked, and tried to be proud that I was working on such a good place as Ransom Ranch.

My Grandpa Leland had been a mail carrier for the Union Army during the Civil War and came out here to Montana when the war was over. His first job was being a ranch-hand. He worked hard and bought some cattle and then bought his own land and more cattle. This was Ma's father, which means Ma was born here and had my little upstairs room when she was a girl. She met my daddy at a corn-husking dance. He was out from Indiana visiting his cousin. He didn't know too much about ranching, being from a farm.

My Pa had never talked much about his boyhood house. He didn't talk too much at all, but we all knew that he loved Ransom Ranch. We knew that by the way he cared for the horses, rubbing their backs after long days at work—or the way he sat with the cows when they were calving—or the way he looked out at the cattle on the pastures or toward the growing wheat. We all knew he loved the place.

It was time to get a snack, a slice of cornbread with honey and a big glass of creamy milk. Just as I was washing my hands in the bucket of cold water we kept by the kitchen door, something caught my eye.

Through the downstairs window, I saw my brothers returning—but they didn't even come to the house. They veered off and took their horses to the further fields, in the direction of the rolling hills. Were they heading off without me? They could have at least asked me to go. My mule Downey could keep up with their horses pretty good.

I left the window and went upstairs to my room. My bright braided rug seemed trying to cheer me up. But my shady room was getting dim. I was done with school and done with work, and there wasn't much time left before supper and sundown. What was I going to do? How was I going to get rid of this hollow feeling?

It was time. Time to go to my place, down the stairs, out the door, across the near fields, and to the west where a small river ran. There, aspens and pines shaded the banks. There, that hollow feeling went away, even if for a little bit.

I came to the grassy bank and I looked across the river. On a big rock right in the middle of the water was a boy. I had never seen him before.

It was quiet as he turned his head and looked at me.

I told him right away: "This is my river."

"You can't own a river," he said straight back. Then he said, "But I know what you mean. It wants to belong to someone." He held out his hand. "The name's Josiah. Want to join me on this here rock?"

I crossed some small rocks and took his hand. I joined him on the big rock.

"Know what this rock is here for?" he asked.

I thought. The quiet settled upon us.

"It's for people who know how to be still," I said.

We smiled at each other. If I had to pick the moment our friendship began, that would be it. I said, "My name's Clara. My family's ranch is just over the hill."

Josiah nodded. "My family has a plot of land too, up

that way." He pointed up toward the left bank.

"How come I've never seen you at school?" I asked.

"I go to the one in Ercil County."

"Why?"

He gave me a funny look. "The teacher there doesn't care so much, if I'm late or whatever." He picked up a pebble from the river bed, getting half his arm soaked.

"Do you have any brothers or sisters?" I asked.

"An older sister. It's just me and her, and my pa."

"Your mama—?"

"When I was six. She—she died." He threw the pebble back into the river. "What family you got?"

"Two older brothers. Caleb and Jacob. Nineteen and seventeen. I'm nine."

"I'm nine too."

"Funny we never met till today," I said.

"Well, maybe it's like the valleys and mountains. We'd have to meet, sooner or later."

My heart gave a little jump. I looked at him more closely. How did he know to say something like that? I started to get that feeling I did when I spotted a four-leafed clover, or found a stray feather in the tall grass, or saw a robin taking flight. "Yeah," I said. "Maybe it's like that."

Josiah kept listening so I kept talking. "I bet your sister is nicer than my brothers. They treat me like something else, always pulling on my braids. That's how I've learned to fight. I can pin almost anyone to the ground, girl or boy. They've taught me. One, two, three!" I stood up on the rock to show him, swinging my arms, my voice getting louder. "And then a kick there!" I kicked hard at imaginary shins.

"Forget about stillness, this rock is for the Lynn, Montana, fighting champion!" Josiah jumped up beside me. "The mighty! The great! Clara—what's your last name?"

"Reese!"

"Clara Reese!"

I cheered. Then laughed. Had I just cheered for myself?

"What do you want to do when you grow up?" Josiah asked.

I thought for a few moments. I thought about Ma's face when she explained the leaves and clouds. Maybe I would be a teacher. Maybe I would be a scientist and know why thunder grumbled and ice made lace on our winter windows.

But then I thought about the river, my river. Sometimes it was brown, like now, or a clear blue, shiny under the noon sky. Sometimes, at sunset, it was near purple. It greeted me every time I came to it. I could be myself here.

"A nurse," I said. "I like finding and helping. What do you want to be?"

Josiah paused. "I'm not sure," he said.

I could tell by the way he spoke that he wanted to say more but was shy. I was going to press him, but I looked up to the sky. The sun was so low I knew I had to go. I stood and shifted from my right foot to my left. How do you say goodbye to a new friend? He looked at me and stood up too. He held out his hand.

"If you shake hands over rock and water, your friendship will be as solid as the rock and as long as the river."

I was about to ask how he knew that was so, but stopped. "I know," I said. We shook hands.

I climbed on the smaller rocks to the right bank. I looked back to the strange boy and waved goodbye.

I ran back to the ranch and got a scolding from Pa about being gone too long. But that night I went to bed with the strange picture in my head of a thin boy on a big rock, his eyes wide and full of ideas.

That was how Josiah and I met.

A Hand-Written Note

The next weeks brought daily prizes, like the beauty of our river and how Josiah and I made each other laugh; and one-time-only prizes, like hidden mountain paths and a visiting missionary family from Brazil. My brothers taught me bar songs that I taught Josiah. We decided that "Sunbonnet Sue" was our favorite. Ma taught me how to make gingersnaps. We kept a tin of them down by our river.

We fished and swam in the afternoons, and Josiah would declare, "It's time for a break, I think." We'd lounge on the bank, munching on our cookies and making up stories. Mine were usually about the Crow or Dakota Indians, or about horses that could fly, but I never knew what Josiah's would be about. He could tell stories about anything. My favorite was about a girl-star named Celeste. She fell in love with the earth, and went through all kinds of escapades to get here.

We found out that we both liked Sundays over Fridays and fried pork rinds more than smoked ribs. Josiah had showed me his favorite spots on the river, and I showed him all my interesting finds, as well as my set of postcards, with pictures of the White House and Old Faithful. Josiah looked so long at the postcard with Old Faithful, I gave it to him. We decided we would visit those places together.

It was funny. I had friends at the schoolhouse, who I talked to and laughed with. But I had never had a friend like Josiah, who I didn't have to talk to, and who was so easy to laugh with. I didn't have to worry about laughing too loud or too long, or not at all. I could take as long as I wanted on a walk, finding all sorts of summer beauties— blooms and birds and raccoon trails. Josiah didn't care about walking slow. Just like our rock and river, our friendship *was* growing solid and long.

I hardly ever felt that hollow feeling anymore.

I wasn't there the first time Josiah met my Ma. I was out doing chores when he came over, and Ma met him at the door. Josiah told me later, "I was so tongue-tied, I forgot to say my name."

"How did Ma know it was you?"

"I told her I was the river boy."

No one in my family could understand why, but my favorite chore on the ranch was tending to the sheep.

"But they smell," Jacob said, one time when he and I were in the kitchen, trying to sneak cookies out from under Ma's eyes. He slyly slid a cookie across the table.

"More than all the other animals put together. And you smell just like them, Clar-o, after you lead them into the pens." He pinched his nose in disgust and pulled my braid. Jacob (Jake the Snake we call him) was my second oldest brother. He was tall and lanky with a mop of reddish-brown curls. Everyone knew he wouldn't stay on the ranch. At first chance, he would be gone, making his way as an automobile mechanic.

About two years earlier, when he visited Ma's aunt in West Virginia, Jacob had seen a Model A Cadillac driving up Charleston's Main Street. After that, he talked of nothing else. His plan was to own the first car in Lynn, Montana. He was a real dandy too, dressing up every Friday night to go into town for a dance, or to shoot pool, or just strut around talking about car parts to impress the girls.

"But I like how sheep are woolly, and I like their eyes," I answered him. "And besides, I don't smell half as bad as you do with your man's perfume."

I was walking among the sheep one day, pretending to be a shepherdess, letting them eat out of my hands and rubbing their wool, when I saw Josiah walking up the lane to my house. I climbed over the fence of the sheep paddock and ran toward the front of the house.

There Josiah was, sitting on the porch. Half of his face was in the shade.

"Hey there, Josiah."

"Hey there, Clara." He stood up. "You remember that forest fire last autumn, on the southwest side of Buntain?" Buntain was a hill about two miles west of Lynn.

"You bet I do. Caleb's friend is on the forest fire brigade, and he had told us all about it. The boys worked hard to keep that fire contained."

"You think any fireweed's growing there?"

"And you know what fireweed means—"

Josiah grinned. "Butterflies."

"Let me get my net."

I ran upstairs and grabbed my butterfly net and my little logbook where I kept track of all the butterflies I'd seen. Of course we needed a canteen of water, two apples, and some slices of cheese. I put it all in my canvas satchel and joined Josiah. He was kicking dirt and looked up at me as I hopped down the porch steps.

"Got some snacks?" he asked.

"What do you think!" I shouted. We raced to the road.

The two-mile walk brought us west, and higher too. At the bottom of Buntain, we found a full-leaved maple to sit under and enjoy our snack. Then we started the ascent in earnest along the fire brigade path. It would take us up the hill and over to the southwest side.

The sun was on our backs. This side of the hill was mostly long, grassy meadows, with some scattered oak trees. How long the view was, and how bright too, with the summer afternoon light.

We weren't talking much. We didn't need to.

We started rounding the path, going more west, coming around to the left. Soon the whole next side of the hill opened out before us.

"Holy smokes," I said.

We stopped and gazed out.

There it was, the long stretch of the burnt-out forest— the black, strangled trunks, the wreckage of old trees. And all through was blooming fireweed, its tall thin stems and bursts of bright, delicate, magenta flames.

"It's kind of scary looking," I whispered. "But it's beautiful too."

Josiah seemed to be taking it in real slow, not missing one blackened tree limb or one pink blossom. "Never seen anything like it."

We entered the scene slowly, careful not to break any of the flowers. The sooty, rotting wood made black scratch marks on our shins.

"Clara, there one goes," Josiah pointed.

A big majestic Monarch butterfly was not five feet away—and beyond fluttered a silky blue moth—and then three yellow ones. "Land sakes!" I cried.

"Gonna get out your net?" Josiah asked.

I didn't really want to run around with all the spiky wood. And I didn't want to crush the flowers. And sometimes, catching butterflies in my net just doesn't suit me. "I'll just log them in my notebook."

Josiah's eyes sparked. "You keep a notebook?"

"Not for writing. Just for logging all the stuff I see, you know, trees, butterflies, spiders. Nice meals. Good checker moves."

Once again it looked like my friend was going to say something—but instead he gasped and pointed. "Cardinals! Male and female—"

I whipped out my book, and the logging began.

"I guess I should have packed a bigger snack."

"Yeah. Like sandwiches or something." Josiah breathed out slowly and waited for me to catch up. "You all right?

"Just hungry as all get out. Don't you dare talk about sandwiches—I'll start thinking about ham and bacon—oh, and those big Ulysses tomatoes from the garden." I nearly fell over thinking about that sandwich. "And we've still got to climb down this hill and *then* we've got two miles more!" I paused. "Josiah, where do you live? Isn't your house between here and my home?"

A funny look came over Josiah's face.

"What?" I asked.

"We can—" he started. "We can go to my place. My house. There's milk and bread there, I think. That will keep us going. You're right. My house is closer to

Buntain."

"Well, thank the Lord for small mercies!" That was one of Ma's favorite sayings, and it seemed to fit our scenario perfectly.

We turned down a dead-end road. I saw a house not too far down on the right, and an old, run-down place way at the end. The house on the right looked nice—not too big, pretty with white shutters and a circle of apple trees.

"That's my place, down there," Josiah said.

I nodded—and swallowed my surprise. The run-down place was a house? *Josiah's* house? My tummy did a strange drop.

We got a bit closer. I could see the house wasn't really run-down, just in need of some repair. It was a tiny place, made of rough, dark wood. There were stables in the back, and beyond that a long, scraggly field. In front of the house was a bent pine, looking so lonely that it hurt me.

"Just—wait a second," Josiah whispered. We stopped by the pine tree. Josiah seemed to be listening for something. All I could hear was the soft, soft wind through the pine needles.

"Well, welcome," Josiah said and led the way to the house. For the first time in my life, I was happy to follow. I walked a few paces behind him as we climbed the rickety steps. Josiah opened the door for me.

We walked into his house, and coming in from the

bright sun, the darkness was thick and heavy. The smell of something stale, like moldy bread, was thick in the air too. I wanted to turn outside and breathe in deep, but I made myself stand there.

Josiah told me to wait there, and he went across the room to lift down a big piece of wood covering the window. There weren't any glass panes, just a big open square. Light and the freshness eased across the room.

To the right of the room was a stove and beside it a sink. On some shelves, dishes were stacked. The way they were stacked, and the way some daisies sat in a cup on the table, and the way the curtains were hemmed with a red ribbon—I could see the handiwork of his sister Lydia.

Josiah poked around the cupboards. He held up two biscuits and a jar filled with sparkling, amber-colored jam. "Lydia made this just last week. Dandelion jelly."

"Oh—I've never had that. I'll have to log it."

"Want to eat, on the way back to your place?"

"No. Let's eat here." I sat down at the wooden table by the window.

Josiah nodded and set out two teacups. They were old and pretty. "Those Lydia's?" I asked.

"They were my mother's. Lydia and I use them on special occasions. Milk?"

"Yes, please. Milk and biscuits, can't beat that."

"Wait till you try this dandelion jelly."

It was sweet tasting, like mild honey. Lydia must be a

nice sister. But something—something wasn't right.

"Where do you sleep, Josiah?"

"Well, when Pa sleeps in the lean-to, I sleep out here. Lydia makes us a pallet. Or if Pa sleeps out here, there's bunk beds in the lean-to."

"Like if your Pa comes home late, from work?"

"Yeah, exactly."

I nodded and looked around. With the window open, the place seemed like a good place for my friend. "Where do you keep all your stuff? You know, books and clothes?" I asked.

Josiah carefully set down his teacup. "That chest over there—" he nodded across the room. "That's all mine."

It was an old wooden chest, made of cherry wood by the look of it. There were two quilts on top of it.

"Hey," Josiah said. "I've got something in there you might want to log. It's a scarlet feather that I found in the back field. It's huge, Clara—I don't know what bird it's from."

"Not an eagle, huh?"

"I think it's too red for that."

We were crossing the room and were at the chest. Josiah handed me the quilts and opened the chest.

I inhaled softly. Inside the chest was the most interesting array of found things I had ever seen. Tacked onto the inside of the lid were a few photographs, some newspaper articles, a piece of dark blue velvet, dried wild flowers, that huge scarlet feather, and a piece of paper that said, in shaky, fancy handwriting, LOOK FOR IT EVERYWHERE.

"Josiah," I whispered. "What are these things?"

We knelt down.

"That's a photo of my mother, when she was sixteen. Lydia was a baby then, but she's not in the photo."

I peered close. The lady had Josiah's round chin and sharp cheeks.

"She's pretty, isn't she?" Josiah asked.

"She's beautiful."

"And that photograph is my pa, when he was still east in Virginia. He's only fourteen then. He worked in the mines there."

I peered close again. A handsome lad, I saw.

"These newspaper clippings are about—they're about writers from Montana. And this blue cloth, it's—well, it's from Ma's casket—"

I was glad I had the quilts in my arms. I held onto them tight.

"And that's the feather that I found, and these wildflowers were just leftover from a dried bouquet that Lydia made for her friend. And, here are my books. They are my prized possession. Lydia and me saved three summers in a row to buy this set through the mail." He pointed to a stack of five books, dark-cloth bound.

"You like books?" I asked.

Josiah sat back. "Yeah, you bet—I mean, you open them, and you're in a new land and hearing funny stories and braving scary things." He ran his hand over the books and seemed to dust them off, but I don't think they were dusty. "You know how you want to be a nurse?"

"Sure."

"I want to be a writer." His eyes got wide as he spoke, "Think of it, Clara. Seeing your ideas typed out for everyone to read."

"What would you write? Stories?"

Josiah moved forward and reached to close the lid. "No. Not stories. Ideas. Like why we do things. Why we like logging unusual finds, or telling about our brothers, or why we keep secrets."

He was just about to close the chest. I had to ask. "And that paper, with the handwriting?"

Josiah looked over at me, waiting.

I asked, "Did your ma write that?"

"She did."

"What did she mean? Look for what everywhere?"

"When she wrote it," Josiah said, "She was kind of far gone already—I mean, her fever was really high. She said a whole bunch of things when she wrote that—like how strangers can be kind, or the way Pa is sometimes— sometimes nice. Or how Lydia makes pretty things, like those curtains. I think—I mean, I'm not sure—but I think she was talking about the way people care. If you look for it, you can see it. You know?"

"Care, like loving? Look for love everywhere?"

Josiah said nothing back, but his eyes took in the idea. He closed the lid of the chest.

We washed the teacups and put the milk in the cool cupboard. Josiah closed the window, and darkness took over the room once again. We left.

We were halfway to my house, when Josiah said, "You know what, Clara, I think that's exactly what she meant."

On the Lookout

When we got to my house, we played about five games of checkers. Josiah beat me at four, which proves my mind was elsewhere. After Josiah left, I walked up to my room. I laid down on the bed.

I was quiet for so long, I wasn't surprised when I heard Ma's footsteps on the stairs.

My mother has always been a soft, strong woman. Her thick red hair had whiffs of white, and on workdays she wore it in a low bun like a knot, but for church and special days, Ma's bun was swirled up, and she looked like a queen. She knew our Ransom Ranch like the back of her hand, and she knew how to work the land, too—she and Pa worked together, side by side, rounding up the cattle or piling the hay.

She knocked on my door, and I said, "Come on in"—but when the words came out, they sounded like a long sigh.

"You all right, Clara?"

"I guess so."

"You thinking things through?" she asked.

I spoke slowly, trying to get into words what I was thinking. "Pretty stuff in ugly stuff—doesn't make the ugly stuff go away."

Ma sat down on my bed. Her warm hand squeezed my ankle. "How did you come up with that thought?"

I sat up and scooted back against the pillows. "Today, we saw fireweed in the burnt-out forest. It was quite a sight, Ma."

"I bet it was—all that bright color with everything that was burned."

"And then Josiah's place. There were such nice things there—Lydia's curtains, and—oh, you should see Josiah's collection of interesting finds. But it was . . . It's just that it was really dark in there too." I kept thinking of my own airy room, with its window facing the mountains and the sunrises and our barn. The quilt on my bed was the color of dandelions. But Josiah wakes up to all those shadows.

Ma squeezed my ankle again.

"Why, Ma?" I asked.

Ma did not answer my question, but she said: "It's hard when someone we care about has less, has been given less. It's very hard, Clara."

Ma's voice sounded sadder than I had ever heard it. She continued, "You know, someone I care about had nothing like Ransom Ranch to grow up in. His house was very different. And you think you can just love him, and everything is all right. But it's not so easy."

Who was Ma talking about? About Pa? My breath caught in my throat.

Ma said, "But Josiah's outside a lot, Clara. And with you."

I considered her words. They didn't seem enough.

Next afternoon, I was working away in the barn. The night before, Pa had asked me to carefully clean out the milk hold. I was just finishing up drying each and every part of the large container. That's when I heard Ma's voice call from house to barn.

"Clara! Josiah is here to see you!"

I glanced quickly over to Caleb, my oldest brother. He was like Pa, brown-haired, tall and stocky. He was pouring a big sack of feed into a trough. Had he heard Ma? I didn't want him to tease me. I watched Caleb stand up, straighten his back, and, before I knew it, he winked at me. Blast.

"Sounds like someone's come calling," he said.

I gave him a hard glare.

"I'm just joking," he huffed, and sauntered off towards the barn.

It's hard to pin things like friendship down, but I think Caleb and me have always been what people call kindred spirits. The way he said things was the way I thought them, like the way he sang "Shenandoah," was just how I heard it in my mind.

I would have barged right through the kitchen door, but I saw Josiah through the window and stopped. He and Ma were sitting at the kitchen table, and he was talking with her in a serious way. I listened through the window, trying to breathe as quietly as I could.

"I try to stay on the lookout for what I can write about," Josiah was saying. "I mean, I listen and watch people. But sometimes it feels like I'm not a *part* of anything, to write about it."

Ma listened. She didn't answer right away. Then she said, "It is hard to see what's right in front of us. But we can write about anything. Even tough things."

"And good things?" I barely heard Josiah's question, he asked it so low.

Ma tilted her head in surprise. "Yes," she replied. "Good things too."

I thought her words made a perfect entrance. "Hello, everybody."

Josiah jumped up out of his chair. "Guess what's come to Lynn?"

"What?" I jumped too.

"A traveling circus! Murray and Bradley."

I whispered in awe, "What?"

"Yes," Josiah nodded. "With monkeys and rope walkers and men who walk through fire and everything! Can you go?"

"Can I go?" I shouted to Ma.

"I don't see why not."

I grabbed Josiah's hands and we sashayed around the kitchen. Well, I sashayed, and dragged Josiah along. "We're going to the circus!" I shouted.

"All right, all right!" Ma said. "Here's some apples for the walk, and here's a little pocket money." She handed us two coins each. Our mouths dropped clear to the floor.

Josiah grabbed her hand and pumped it up and down. All shyness was gone. "Thank you, *ma'am*," he said. "See?" he asked, looking up at her, "Got to be on the lookout for those good things."

The screen door slammed behind us as Ma called out, "I'll have Caleb pick you up!"

There was something funny about her voice. It was sad and happy. I looked back. I couldn't really see her through the screen.

"We won't be fit for the ranch, Ma! We'll have to join the circus!"

We ran for awhile and then walked, and wondered what kind of person you have to be to jump through fire and play with gravity.

The Magician and the Idea

The circus was louder and bigger and wilder than I had imagined it would be. The clowns tumbled, and the trapeze artists flew through the air. They were my favorite. I pictured myself way up high, covered in purple, being flung from one pair of arms to another. I decided that with the help of my brothers, I would have no problem.

"What's your favorite?" I asked Josiah above the din of cheers and whistles. He sat next to me with a lollipop in one hand and a candied apple in the other.

"The candied apple!" he said. "The trapeze people, too."

"And the monkeys!" I shouted back.

With the music and the sights and my new best friend beside me, my first circus was better than beating Jake at checkers.

"Mind if we sit here?" an old lady asked Josiah.

"No, ma'am. Have a seat."

The old lady turned to an older man standing on the

steps behind her.

"Timothy!" she called. "We can sit here!"

He moved toward her, and they sat down together. They held hands and took turns biting out of the same candied apple.

I stared. I didn't know adults ate candied apples.

"See, it's like my ma's note," Josiah whispered to me, "You can see so clear how that old man and lady care for each other."

"It's true," I replied. "Like the way my pa brushes our horses. If I told you about that, I wouldn't need to say the word *care*. You would just know."

"And how about this boy!"

Josiah and I both jumped in our seats.

"How about it, sonny?"

A man in a flaming red jacket and a long floppy hat stood before us. "Want to help the magician with his next act?" he asked Josiah.

We both gasped. Josiah was speechless.

"Yes!" I yelled back. "Yes, he does!" I shoved Josiah forward.

"A round of applause for our plucky lad!" the floppy-hat man yelled. I cheered like crazy.

Josiah walked into center circle of the circus tent.

The floppy-hat man took Josiah over before the magician, who stood beside a tall, black box.

The magician, swirling his red satin cape, spoke to us

in a deep voice. "I will make this boy disappear before your very eyes!" He spun the box around to prove there were no trick doors or hidden boxes. We clapped like mad, especially since one of us stood up there.

Josiah stepped inside the box. Just before the magician closed the curtain, Josiah found me in the audience. His smile got even wider.

The magician dropped the red, plush curtain and we stared, holding our breaths.

"Voila!" He opened the curtain, and Josiah was gone! The audience clapped, I jumped around, the curtain closed again, the magician waved, we held our breath once more, the curtain opened . . .

There stood Josiah. He was decked out with a long, glittering cape. He bowed for us.

Among the noise and frenzy, something strange happened. Just before Josiah took off his cape and returned to his seat, the magician began waving his wand again, bringing it down over Josiah. Extra magic, or something. But the way Josiah jerked back when the wand came toward him sent chills down my spine. What did it remind me of?

I didn't like what I remembered. The summer before, an old black lab came around our house from a nearby ranch. Every time I tried to pat it, it would jerk away. Pa said it was because its owner was rough to it.

"Clara! Clara!" Josiah was running back toward our

seats. "I got the idea! What I've been waiting to know!"

I stared at him. "What are you talking about?" I asked. "You just disappeared, Josiah! You were *in* the circus!"

"My idea for my book!" He scooted past the people on our row and plopped down beside me.

"What do you mean, your idea?"

"When I was standing behind that false wall, hiding. The magician whispered to me what to do. That's when I got my idea." He looked at me. "We can write a book about people. Like that couple." He pointed his thumb to the old couple beside us. "Like the way your pa looks after your horses. And not just our own ideas, but we would ask around. Anyone could be a part of it."

"But that's not a story," I said.

"Books don't have to be stories, Clara. Or at least not one story about the same people, beginning to end. They will all run together—my story, your story—all the stories. They'll all come together like our river. That's how our book will be. What do you think?"

I wasn't so sure, but then I thought of a small photograph Ma has, where she's sitting beside her grandma's ma, who was as old as Moses the last time Ma visited home. "It'll be like a photograph or painting, won't it?"

"We can do it together. It will be the best book in the world."

I got that, no problem. "The best book in the world!"

I shouted. A circus is a good place for that kind of outburst.

"There you two are!" We heard a voice above us and looked up. It was Caleb.

"I've come to take you home," he said. He held out his hand to Josiah. "You must be Josiah. I'm Caleb."

Josiah shook his hand, but his face got red and white in patches. He looked away with shyness.

We left the big red circus tent. The night suddenly seemed so quiet. The air was cool, and the sky was dark. Four little stars were shining through the clouds.

"Now, Josiah," Caleb said as we climbed into the wagon, "Tell me where you live, and we'll drop you off."

"Don't worry about it," Josiah said quickly. "You can just drop me off at Harvey Road. It's halfway between home and your place."

I thought Caleb would argue, but to my surprise, he just nodded. The ride home was quiet except for the soft hoof beats of our horse Dakota. Caleb stopped at the corner of Harvey Road and shook hands with Josiah, just like I was hoping he would. I leaned over the side of the wagon and whispered as he walked away, "The best book in the world, River Boy."

Josiah smiled and waved goodbye.

So Gentle and So Fiery

I was halfway up the stairs when I heard Caleb ask Ma and Pa a question. It was about Josiah.

"Do you know who Josiah's father is?" Caleb asked.

"I do. I recognized him right away." Ma's voice floated up to where I sat on the stairs.

"It's Fry," Caleb answered. "Old Jim Fry."

"Jim Fry?" Pa sounded mad. "You knew Clara was with Jim Fry's son, Violet?"

Ma answered sharp, "Of course I knew, Frank."

It got quiet.

Pa spoke again, his tone soft: "I'm sorry. It's just…"

I heard some movement. I think Ma reached for Pa's hand.

"Did Josiah say anything?" Ma asked.

Caleb said, "He didn't need to. His face gave him away. He looks just like his older sister. Lydia. She went to school with Jake and me. It's funny. She never let me take her home either."

"I remember her," Pa replied. "She made it into the

university, didn't she?"

"Yes, sir." Caleb's voice lowered. "Didn't go, though. Not with her little brother to take care of. And the way Old Fry drinks." Caleb's voice lowered more. I strained to hear. "Lydia and I got to be pretty good friends in school. We did a history project together, and a few nights we went to the school library in Ercil County."

It got quiet again. I waited for someone to speak so I could move up the stairs. I needed to think, about Josiah and Lydia and Old Jim Fry—

"Lydia's not flashy-pretty, you know, but she is kind of beautiful. Did you ever know that Jacob took a real fancy to her? He was always talking about how light her eyes were." He paused for a moment. "It is true I never saw someone be so gentle and so fiery at once." Caleb chuckled. "Anyways, Jake was crazy about her."

When he finished no one said a word. I heard Pa unfold the newspaper.

I crept upstairs, a bright idea sprouting in my heart. My idea would help Josiah and his sister and even our best book in the world. Josiah needed help, and this book would do it.

The Best Book in the World

Next morning after chores, I ran to the river. Ma was going to need my help that day because she was making cheese, so I knew I'd have to talk fast—not a problem for me.

"Josiah!" I yelled when I saw him on the rock. I knew he would be waiting there. He looked up at me, eyes bright.

"Clara! We've got to get started on our best book in the world." He reached out his arm to help me up, and that's when I saw it. There was a nasty-looking bruise above his elbow. I stopped quickly.

"What happened?" I asked, even though down deep I already knew.

He shook his head and said nothing. I climbed up on the rock beside him. It was as quiet as when we first met. But this time the river was clear blue.

Josiah pulled out a worn notebook. "Okay. The question is, how do we get everybody's ideas for our book?"

"But if everyone else writes it, we won't be the authors."

"We'll be the editors," he explained. "We'll sort through everyone's ideas and write about them." He shifted to his knees. "But we have to figure out how to get everyone's ideas."

"How about we go around asking people, like at the pharmacy, or go to their homes?" I asked.

Josiah squirmed. "I don't know. You'd have to do all the talking."

"That's okay."

"But—won't it seem like—they don't have a choice to say something? We want stories that people *want* to tell us."

"You leave that to me. Pa says I'd make a good salesman, when I'm trying to convince him to let me do something."

Josiah's shrug was followed by a grin. "Where should we start?"

"A girl Lucy at school invited me over to her place— let's go there tomorrow, right after chores."

"Sounds good. Now, tell me what you're so excited about."

My mouth dropped open. "How did you know?"

"I saw you running to our rock. I knew you had something to tell me."

"Okay, listen," I crouched down on the rock and

spoke in a whisper, though no one was around. "Last night I heard my brother, Caleb, talking about your sister—"

"My sister?" Josiah's eyes widened. "Why?"

"He knew Lydia from school. Anyway, Jake *likes* Lydia. It gave me an idea. What if we try and get Jake and Lydia together? You know, get a good story for our book."

"Jake likes her?"

"Caleb said he did."

"But how could we do it?"

"That's what I was thinking," I said. "Let's somehow reunite them. We could do it easy. I bring Jake; you bring Lydia. We meet at Miss Tilly's. And when they start talking, about school and the ranch and music, they'll remember how they liked each other. It will be a great story."

Josiah was staring at the water with a funny look. Didn't he like my idea? Then he said quickly, "That's a good idea. I mean, it's good for Lydia. It will be all right."

There was a sad look in his eyes.

"We don't have to do that right away," I said quickly. "Let's see how our story-collecting goes. Then, if and only if we need to, we can get Jake and Lydia to meet."

"Now that sounds all right. Only if we need to."

I wanted to tell him more of my idea, that if our book did well, he could take all the money. Then things would be better for him and Lydia. But I didn't want to say my plan just yet. I didn't want to raise his hopes in case the book went bad. I glanced to the sky. "I've got to get home. I'm helping Ma make the cheeses."

He nodded at me. We climbed off the big rock and onto the smaller ones below.

"I'll see you tomorrow!" We turned our ways, him to the left, and me to the right.

"Clara—wait!"

He scrambled back to our rock. "I almost forgot to show you this picture."

I stepped back to the rock and looked into his hand, at the object he held there. It was another picture of his mother, this one when she was older. A baby was on her lap.

"That's you, isn't it?"

"Yes."

We both looked at the picture again.

"You remember her any?"

"Kinda. Sometimes when Lydia bakes something, I think I can. And there's a place in our garden that makes me think of her. I think my ma was like your ma. You know, with that way of listening."

A Thorn and a Marvel

A puzzle was growing in my mind. It sprang up from different places. It was mostly about Josiah, but about Pa too.

I had planned to talk to Caleb about it, but somehow that afternoon came together for me to talk to the one person I needed to.

I was pretending to be the sheep's shepherdess. The day was a majestic July day, with a pearl-gray sky that looked purple at the edges and the meadows almost white against it. I saw Pa walk into the barn with a cow that had a slight limp.

"Clara!" he called to me. "Come give me a hand."

I ran into the barn, the cool shadows darkening my sight for a second.

"What happened?" I asked, joining him in one of the stalls.

"This lady has a big thorn in her hoof." He patted her side. "I saw her limping out in the field. I don't think it will hurt to pull it out, but you just put your hand on her head to steady her."

"Sure." I loved helping out with the animals. I felt like a nurse, like Clara Barton, starter of the Red Cross. I put my hand on her cheek and tried to look into her eyes, to tell her it was okay.

It was quiet in the barn except for the tiny wind coming through the doors and the noise of Pa's rummaging through his tools.

The words came out before I knew it. "Pa, do you remember that dog that came by, last summer? The one that crouched down every time we tried to pet it?"

Pa gently picked up the cow's back right hoof. He looked up at me.

"Yes, I do."

"I saw . . . I mean . . . Do you think that if a person did that, they'd do it for the same reason?"

I saw Pa clench and unclench the tool in his hand. "You saw someone move that way?" he asked.

I bit my lip. "Yeah. I think so." The light from the door made a square around our feet. It made shines and shadows on Pa's face and his gray-blue eyes. "At the circus. Josiah kind of moved like that, when the circus man was bringing a wand over his head."

Pa slowly dug out the dirt from the cow's hoof. "I think I know what you mean," he said in a real low voice. "Josiah is probably not safe in his own home."

I looked at the cow's face between my hands. She

stared at me with her large eyes. I looked at her as I spoke. "You know, after Josiah and I say goodbye, and I come home . . ." I searched for the words. Pa waited. "I feel *thick*, like I've got too much of something. Too much family, too much food . . ."

Pa gently pried away at the hoof. "Keep your hand on her, gentle-like. You know, Clara, that being *thick*, as you call it, might actually come from looking in the wrong direction."

"How do you mean, Pa?"

"Truth is, *you* haven't done much to deserve the life you live. You do have some choices. Do your chores or not. Be kind or not. And when you get older, the choices you make will be bigger. But a lot of what goes on now doesn't have much to do with you. Same goes for Josiah. Much of what he lives with isn't *his* doing. So if you're looking at what you have or he hasn't, you're not really looking at *him*, or his choices, or his plans."

Pa sighed again and spoke a little softer. "Thing is, I had a childhood a lot like Josiah's."

His words filled the barn. They pressed against my heart.

He spoke again, "When I first heard you were friends with Jim Fry's son, I didn't like it. It just seems that if you keep doors shut, they're shut then." Pa concentrated on the thorn. "But that's not all doors are for, are they?"

The cow shifted uneasily. I held her face tight.

Pa said, "Just a few more seconds . . ."

He held up the thorn for me to see. It was about two inches long.

"No wonder this girl was limping!" I said, patting her head.

Pa stood up and swung the stool back to its peg. "You're a good friend, Clara. I'm glad you care enough to hurt. But don't just feel bad. It's not fair. It's not fair for your friendship with Josiah. Friendship is *joy* in another person, and a person is always more than their hurt. A friend is a gift and a marvel. You don't have to measure what they have or don't have, because at the end of the day, a friend gives himself, or herself, to you. And you give yourself back."

Pa and I led the cow out of the barn. The pearly, white sunshine warmed our faces.

"Thanks, Pa."

He nodded. I watched him walk on toward the field, the cow trailing behind with just a slight limp.

I knew more of my father, and the weight of his words surrounded me.

Gumption at Lenwood Farm

The sun was lying low and lazy as Josiah and I set out toward Lucy's place. We could get to Lenwood Farm through town, but we decided to take the long way around, alongside a lost-and-found brook. The mountains, like kings and queens in velvet robes, were behind us. Gold-green meadows stretched out all around, with a few oaks marking the horizon. A soft June wind was blowing from the west.

It seemed like a good day for collecting stories. But like Pa said, "What seems to be" is often a setup for surprise.

We finished the last verse of "Land from the Sky-Blue Water" just as we reached Lenwood Farm's big wooden fence. I unlatched it, and the two of us rode the fence as it swung open. "Yee-haw!" I cried.

"You know what you're going to say?" Josiah asked, as we re-latched the fence.

Hmm. I hadn't really thought that through. "The

words will come," I said. "Depends on who's all there."

Josiah shook his head slightly. I saw he was a bit nervous.

We were just rounding a little wood of birch trees, when I heard four voices call my name. I looked up. Climbing trees, way up high, were Lucy, Jackson, Peter, and Meredith.

"Hey-ho!" I greeted them. "Nice day for climbing birches."

"Watcha doin' here, Clara?" Jackson asked. "We haven't seen you all summer. Meredith said she seen you with some new boy in town."

"I seen her with this here boy at Miss Tilly's," Meredith said. They all started climbing down, and circled around us. "I saw them through the window."

"This here is Josiah," I said. "He goes to the school in Ercil, but he lives on the north side of Lynn."

"Why you go to Ercil?" Jackson asked. "Lynn not good enough for you?"

I sucked in my breath and waited for Josiah's answer. He shrugged, his face getting red. "My Pa gets on easier with the schoolmaster." Josiah's voice was a little shaky.

"Well, how you fellows been?" I asked. We all started walking on the path to the house.

"Jackson's pig had a whole new set of piglets," Meredith said. "We've been looking after them, getting paid for it. A cent each week."

We were walking toward the paddock and stables and just reached the shade from the pine trees around the house. It was cooler as we walked into the shadows.

"What brings you over our way, anyhow, Clara?" Lucy asked. "We were thinking you were too good for us. But now I see you just got a *beau*."

I stopped dead in my tracks. "Josiah is not my beau. He's my new friend."

"If he's not your beau, then you don't really like him," Lucy taunted back.

"Of course I like him. He's my new friend."

"You just feel bad 'cause he don't have any friends in Lynn!" Jackson added.

I waved my fist in front of Jackson's face. "Ain't true—ain't at all!" I could feel anger starting to pump through me.

"Clara—" Josiah started, but he was cut off by Meredith's chants, *"Clara's got a be-au!"*

"He AIN'T my beau!" I shouted.

"Then you don't like him!" Peter shouted back.

"I DO like him!"

"Clara—" Josiah started again, but this time he was cut off by Lucy.

"Prove it, then."

"Fine," I said, my hand still in a fist. "Just tell me how."

"Go to the barn and stomp in some horse dung."

I stared at her. "Have you lost your mind, Lucy?"

"I haven't lost anything. *You've* lost your nerve, if you can't prove that Josiah's your friend and not your beau."

"I'll step in all the horse dung you got in that barn." I swiveled around and marched off. Josiah caught up with me. "Clara, this is stupid. You don't have to stomp in that stuff. I know I'm your friend."

"These hooligans don't, and I won't put up with their antics."

"But stepping in horse muck *is* putting up with it."

"Ah, Josiah, let me be. I know these kids."

Josiah gave me a bewildered look but stuck by my side as I walked into the barn. I blinked in the darkness. The other kids joined us.

"There," said Lucy, pointing to the left. "In those stables, all four of them."

"Right," I said. I went into the first stable. There was a big pile of green-brown mush. I looked around at all of them. I could tell they didn't believe I would do it.

"Here goes," I said, and I stomped, with both feet, right into the pile. It squished all around my boots.

Exclamations came from all sides. "Lordy, Clara," gasped Lucy. "I didn't think you'd really do it."

"Show me to the other stables," I said, head held high. Josiah's bewildered look had changed to one of pride. "No," he said. "I'll do the next one!" He rushed ahead, and nearly jumped on the greeny pile in the next stable. It squished between his toes, and we all squealed in disgust.

I did the next stable, and Josiah finished with the last.

"There," I said, standing beside Josiah. We hooked elbows. "You can believe what you want to, but we proved it."

Lucy lifted her haughty nose. "I guess so," she said—but Jackson slapped me on the back. "I never seen anyone take to a dare so well."

"Well, if you've got a pail—" I lifted my nasty boot. "I can wash off."

Meredith ran over with a pail, and we sloshed some water from the trough into it. I let Josiah go first, since he had bare feet. Then I put fresh water in, and stuck my foot down into the bucket.

I tried to turn it. "Uh-oh," I whispered.

"What's the matter?"

"Nothing." I tried to gently shake my foot, so that no one would notice.

"Clara," Peter said. "Have you got your foot stuck in that pail?"

"I don't—think so—" I lifted my foot. The pail was stuck tight. I shook my foot out in front of me. The pail jingled in front of everybody. "Oh darn it," I cried. "It *is* stuck."

All five burst out laughing—even Josiah. I hobbled around in a circle—up, down, up down—and sang in a loud voice, "OH—I've got poo on my boots, and my boot's stuck in a pail!" I had everyone rolling.

All of the sudden, Lucy shot up straight, face scared. "Oh no."

"What's the matter?" I said. "Want a pail too?"

"I heard my brothers coming back."

We all got real still.

"Presley and Wyatt are here?" I whispered.

"Presley and Wyatt are here," Lucy whispered back. "They went trail-blazing up the hills. And now they're back."

"Who are they?" Josiah asked.

Peter answered, "They're the meanest bullies you ever saw—"

"Clara, they can't see you like this. They just *can't.*"

I heard a horse's neigh not far from the barn.

"What are we going to do?" Meredith wailed softly.

"Everyone, sit in a circle," Josiah said. "Get that horse blanket," he commanded Jackson. Jackson threw Josiah the blanket. "Everyone put your legs out, and put the blanket—there—over us. We're playing rock-paper-scissors, stakes on who gets—who gets—" Josiah was running out of ideas.

"—Grandma's cookies," Lucy breathed. "She just baked a batch today."

Just as Lucy said that, two shadows walked into the barn door. Then the two people who made the shadows. I was so busy pretending to watch Jackson and Josiah play rock-paper-scissors, I didn't look up. But my heart was pounding hard. If they saw that pail—they would tease me mean. My school friends might not be very close to me, but they were all right. Presley and Wyatt, though? I would have never, ever stepped in horse poo to prove something to them.

"What are you losers doing in here?" Presley snarled at us.

Lucy blinked up at him. She spoke in a real laid-back voice. "Hey there, Presley. Wyatt. We're just using the shade to play some rock-paper-scissors. Winner gets Grandma's cookies."

"Like heck he does. I'm getting them."

"Okay, Presley," Jackson said. "We'll find another prize."

"Prize this," Wyatt said, and held up a dead prairie dog. "Shot me this just two hours ago. Might make a good stew."

"You know prairie dog tastes like rat," Peter said. I tried to tell Peter with my glaring eyes to SHUT UP.

"Huh." Wyatt squatted down, his big boots close to me. "You don't like rat, little Peter?"

"I guess it's okay."

"Why are you all covered up with a horse blanket anyway?" Presley asked.

Oh, man. I thought he was too stupid to notice. I was wrong. I looked at the others. Panic was in all our eyes.

"Ya'll are the dumbest kids—you know how hot it is today?" Presley leaned forward, reaching out to pick the blanket up. I decided it was now or never—I grabbed the blanket and threw it in Presley's face.

"RUN!" I shouted, bolting up. "SPREAD OUT!"

All five of us went screaming and running. I was running with a crazy limp, because my right foot was stuck in a pail. Up—down—up—down. The land in front of me seemed to bounce.

Most of us went in all different directions—Lucy toward the mountains, Meredith to the house, the boys to the orchard. I took off to the meadows. I wasn't sure where Josiah had gone.

I glanced back. My stomach flipped over. Presley was running after me. I was panting, and my squeezed foot was starting to throb. Worst thing, I knew a stream was coming up. I was going to be trapped.

I heard Presley's yells now. He was yelling something about a pail-foot. Oh, and I had thrown that horse blanket in his face.

I could hear the stream now. It wasn't more than a hundred feet away. Just as I was going to despair, I glanced back again—and I saw come flying through the air a huge green apple, right at Presley's head.

That apple landed right on the top of Presley's noggin. He stopped and looked around, dazed.

It was Josiah, with Jackson and Peter and Lucy. They

had a basket of apples, and they starting pelting Presley with them.

Presley was going to take after them—when a voice rang out loud and clear from the house. We all looked over.

It was Lucy's grandma, Grandma Toots. A short, spry, strong old lady, she was standing on the porch, one hand on her hip, and the other hand holding Wyatt by the ear. She shouted at Presley to get away from us kids and back to the barn to take care of his horse. "Or else I will be the one riding your horse—for the rest of summer!"

Presley turned to all of us, but he soon bent over, hands on his knees. His shoulders were shaking. How angry *was* he?

But when he looked up, his face was twisted with laughter. "I ain't never seen anything so funny as that girl running around with that pail on her foot. You guys are the strangest people in Lynn!" He ran toward the house and started caring for his horse. Grandma Toots let go of Wyatt's ear. We waited for both the big boys to go into the barn before we walked to the house.

Grandma Toots was standing on the porch, arms crossed.

"Did I see you bruising those gorgeous green apples?"

We nodded slowly.

"Clara Reese," she said. She looked me up and down. "What have you been *doing?*"

I had one boot covered in horse manure and the other foot stuck in a pail. I hobbled up the porch, foot banging with each step. "Grandma Toots, Josiah and I are putting together a book, and we came to ask you to help. What can you tell us about love? Do you have a story? A favorite memory? How would you define love?"

For once, Grandma Toots was at a loss for words. She just stared at me.

I bit my lip.

Then, Grandma burst out laughing—a long, deep, hearty laugh. "Good Lord, Clara Reese, you have gumption. But you can't go around asking people those questions. It's like asking them to take their clothes off. I don't know what you and this Josiah are up to," she nodded kindly at Josiah, and he nodded back, "But you come inside. I'll help you with your pail dilemma, and you can all have some cold milk and warm toast. That's all you'll get from me today, Miss Reese, about the ways of love. You scalawags."

We started trooping in—though I needed to take off my soiled boot first. I sat down on the porch step and untied the laces.

Josiah sat beside me.

"Don't say it," I said.

"You asked all the right questions," Josiah said.

"But Grandma Toots is right, isn't she?" I said. "It *is* like asking people to take their clothes off." I stood up.

"Anyhow, at least we won't have to ask Presley and Wyatt what they think about love. I bet they don't even know how to spell it."

"I don't know," Josiah said, thoughtful-like. "Their answers might be pretty interesting. Still—we'll come up with something, won't we? A way to get people to answer us?"

"You bet we will," I said. We stepped inside Grandma Toot's house. It was cool and bright, and the voices from the kitchen sounded cheery. I saw how Josiah glanced around. It was so very different from his house, with the lonely pine tree.

We had to get our stories about love. We had to find a way to make Josiah's book happen.

Feeling Like a Fool

We sat on our rock for awhile.

"We did say we'd do it," Josiah said slowly. "If we needed to. For the book. And not just for the book. For Lydia."

"You mean, Jake and Lydia meeting?"

Josiah looked at me. "Yes."

"Oh, Josiah—it will be okay. I think it's a perfect idea. Once people get a whiff of real romance, there won't be any stopping them! Everyone will want to tell us their own little story." I leaned over, and put my tummy on the warm rock, letting my hands drape down into the cold water. "All we have to decide is how to pull it off. How late is Miss Tilly's open?"

"It's summertime—she's open till nine o'clock."

"Then let's meet at eight. Late enough to be, you know, dreamy-eyed, but give them plenty of time to talk."

Josiah rested on his tummy too, and stretched his hands down into the river. Our hands looked different underneath the water. "And then they'll get talking . . . and

. . . he'll ask her out for another ice cream?"

"Exactly. Soon she'll be coming over for dinner on Sunday. They'll sit in the parlor, on those awful horse-hair settees, making eyes at each other. Does Lydia like cars, by any chance?"

"I don't think so. I don't think she knows much about them."

"Well, she will soon."

Josiah flashed his hand in front of my face, and water hit my face.

"Hey!" I cried, and scooped up a whole handful of water in his direction.

He shouted and sat up, shaking water from his hair. "Good Lord, what retaliation!"

I laughed. That sounded like something I'd say.

"Okay, then," he said. "Tomorrow's Friday. Tomorrow at 8 pm. Miss Tilly's."

I was so excited about our plans, I didn't really think them through. How was I supposed to get my brother there, anyway?

At seven o'clock, I noticed that Jake the Snake was starting his going-to-town regime—polishing boots, shaving face, dumping cologne all over his clothes.

I stood beside him as he polished his boots on the porch.

"Want something to drink?" I asked. "Some coffee or

tea?"

Jake looked at me like I was crazy. I didn't blame him.

I tried again. "Nice night for an ice cream, wouldn't you say?"

"Nicer night for some pool."

Hmmm. I guess there's nothing like being direct. "Will you take me to Miss Tilly's? I'll treat for some ice cream."

Jake stopped polishing his boots and looked at me again. "Are you kidding me? Ask Caleb."

"Caleb—Caleb doesn't like ice cream like you do. I like enjoying ice cream with people who really like it."

"Ask your beau then."

"Darn it, Jake, for the last time—Josiah's *not* my—" I swallowed. Getting angry at him wasn't going to get him to Miss Tilly's. "We can just go for a little bit. Then I'll walk home, and you can go to the pool hall."

"No thanks, little sister. No babysitting for me tonight."

I pushed my face right close to his. "If you don't go, I'll tell Pa that Caleb's been doing your night chores all this last week."

Jake just kept polishing his shoes. Then he looked at me, and said in a cool voice, "How did you find out about that?"

"I might be annoying, but I'm not stupid."

Jake laughed. "I guess not. Well played, then. I'll go to Miss Tilly's. Better get your sweater, though. You'll be walking back alone, and it gets cold these summer nights."

"What a gentleman you are," I said. For a second I thought that throwing Jake at Lydia might not be so nice for her, but for the sake of Josiah's book, a story like this would get the whole town talking. Trudge on, soldier, I told myself. Trudge on.

It was past 8 o'clock when we were finally walking up Main Street. The whole way there, we had walked as slow as molasses, because my amazing brother didn't want to get his shoes dusty.

I could see Miss Tilly's up ahead. It looked real pretty, with warm lanterns shining from inside. Miss Tilly even had a gramophone playing, a slow sweet song that sounded just perfect for eating ice cream on a summer night. My frustration with Jake eased away—maybe this evening would go as planned, after all.

As we got closer, I could see Josiah and Lydia through the window. Oh—my heart skipped one—how sweet they looked, sitting there, waiting. Josiah had combed his hair in a way I hadn't seen before. And Lydia seemed lovely, poised by the window in a light blue dress.

I heard Jake's sharp intake of air. "What's she doing here?"

"Oh—do you know her?" I tried to ask innocently. "That's Josiah's sister, I think. Lydia—"

"Lydia Fry," Jake finished. But he didn't sound happy.

In fact, he sounded angry. He stopped and said, "What are you playing at, Clara? I'm not going in there."

"Oh no, you've got to, Jake. They're waiting." I reached for his hand. "Please, Jake. It would just be mean, now."

He shook his head. "You planned this, didn't you?"

I stammered—I couldn't figure out what was wrong. "I thought—Caleb said something about how you liked her. I thought—"

"You didn't think at all, Clara! You heard Caleb say something, and you came up with some grand scheme, huh?"

I glanced back to the window. Josiah was waving.

"Jake, Josiah's seen us. He's seen you."

Jake glanced at the window too. He let out a long sigh and cursed.

"I can't go in there, Clara. Caleb was right. I did really like Lydia once, but she—she asked me not to see her again—she didn't—" My brother's face screwed up tight.

"Oh, no," I whispered. "I'm sorry. I'm so sorry, Jake, I didn't know."

"You didn't, did you? You don't know much, little girl."

Now he was making me angry. I did know something. I knew that I needed to help my friend write his blasted book.

I was scared to glance back to the window. Had Lydia

seen him?

"What should I do?"

"Look," Jake handed me some pennies. "You go in and treat for ice cream. If she asks, just say that I walked you here, but have a pool table with the boys lined up at the hall."

He sighed and turned away. He was muttering something about me being an idiot. Or him being an idiot. Or Lydia being an idiot.

I felt heavy and sad and angry all at once. Really, I felt like a fool. I stood in the street, not sure what to do.

I heard the door slam and turned around. Josiah was running over to meet me.

"Where'd your brother go?

"Did Lydia see him?"

"I don't think so."

"Thank goodness. I'll tell you later what happened."

"Everything okay?"

"Besides feeling like a fool?"

"I thought Caleb said Jake *liked* Lydia."

"Did she know anything about our plan?"

"I just told her that we were meeting you. She's excited to meet you. Been hearing about you all summer."

I nodded and smoothed down my flyaway hair. I wished I could smooth my flyaway spirits.

The little bell jingled as we walked in. Lydia turned around.

I tried not to gasp. Her eyes and their expression, like a friendly frown, were so much like Josiah's. She had just the same light brown eyes, the same colored soft brown hair. She seemed a little sad, and in another way, strong and solid. A lot like my friend.

She gave a smile. "I guess Jake wasn't in the mood for ice cream."

"Oh—" My voice trembled. I grimaced to Josiah.

"Oh no, Clara—don't worry about it," Lydia said, putting her hand on my shoulder. "He was only being kind. Let's, the three of us, enjoy our ice cream, and then—how about it—we can go catch fireflies. I brought jars." She held up a blue canvas bag.

I smiled. A collector. A girl after my own heart.

By the time we all said goodnight, I could tell she and Josiah were close. That they were very important to each other. Somehow, seeing her was like finding the source of a river, or maybe like seeing the sheet music of a favorite song. No wonder Josiah hadn't liked the idea of her getting hitched and leaving him.

I unscrewed the lid of my little jar and dropped in the fireflies. Collecting things always makes me feel at ease. But still, there was a part of me starting to panic—how were we going to get people to tell their love stories now? How were we going to write this book?

Sunday Dinner

We were back at our rock. The river waters were flowing clear and cold, and the leaves on the trees fluttering with extra verve, especially the delicate aspen leaves. The sky overhead was a strong blue—a blue that only the summer brings.

Josiah squirmed around before getting comfortable. "I think if we go around asking for stories, people will answer even if they don't want to. Like I said, we want our book to be filled with stories that *want* to be there. The question is—how?"

"What about an ad in the newspaper?" I asked. That idea had come to me late the night before.

"I like it! Then the people who tell their story will have *wanted* to."

"And we'll get lots of mail!" I never got mail, except from Ma's aunt in West Virginia.

"Do we have money for the ad?" Josiah asked.

"I've got some leftover from our circus money."

Josiah took nearly an hour writing our ad, but once it was done, we took it to the newspaper office. It was at the east end of Main Street, so Josiah and I walked through our town, passing by the tall wooden church, sleepy on a Thursday; the taverns, just starting to open their doors; and my schoolhouse, old and quiet in the summer. The office was a small, dark-wood building with a low-eaved porch and a big window painted with the words, *The Lynn Coaster: A Fine Newspaper*. Through the window, I saw a couple men working.

Josiah walked up and pulled on the door. It was locked. We knocked and waved at the two people we could see through the window. One of the men bustled over, keys in hand.

The door opened. A man with a thick crop of dark curls stuck out his head.

"What can I do you for?" he asked in a hurried, though not unkind, way.

Josiah stood tall. "We've come to submit an ad for the paper."

"What edition?"

Josiah paused. "This coming Sunday."

The man opened the door wider. "Sorry the door was locked. The boss isn't here—he's at another convention in Helena until next week—so he asked me to keep the door locked *even* if we were here, mind you. That Dr. Lowell is a strange man, but no point not following orders."

"You're new in town?" I asked, as we walked in and looked around. I've never seen a place so tidy, or bare-bones.

"How'd you guess? Been here two months."

I had figured it by how funny he spoke—kind of sharp and fast. "Oh, we all know how particular Dr. Lowell is about this place." I nodded to the other man in the room, a young man I recognized from Jake's ring of friends. "Billy," I said.

"Hey there, Clara." Billy had a pencil stuck behind his ear. It certainly made him look official, but it didn't fool me. I knew this boy was a wild one, riding white-water rapids in summer or sliding down icy rooftops in winter. Billy nodded toward the new man in town—"This here is Mr. Bertie Jameson, from Boston. Dr. Lowell brought him out here especially for the summer—said he didn't trust us Lynn folk to run the paper while he's at these conventions."

"How do you do, Mr. Jameson," I held out my hand, and Mr. Jameson shook it just like he would an adult, strong and sturdy. I liked this man. "Well, here's our ad," I said, and Josiah brought out the sheet of paper from his notebook.

"Please," Josiah said, "Keep it just as it is. The ad's exactly how we want it."

The man scanned the page. I held my breath. Would he laugh?

He looked up with a warm grin. "Looks dandy. It will come out this Sunday, just as you ordered." He told us the price, we settled up, and waved goodbye. I left the building—and our ad—with a few butterflies in my tummy. It was like letting a secret out into the wide, wide open.

When Ma heard about our ad coming out on Sunday, she invited Josiah for dinner that day. Josiah was delighted, but it didn't sound like the best plan to me. My brothers better not tease me—about Josiah or about the ad.

Around two o'clock Sunday, Josiah knocked on our front door.

"I'll get it!" I yelled. I ran to the door and swung it open.

Josiah had on long dark pants and a white collared shirt. He looked taller, and for a moment, I didn't know what to do. Then he flashed his grin and held out some violets. "These aren't for you. They're for your mother."

It was all back to normal.

I took the violets and led him into our family room where Pa and Jake were. Pa stood up and held out his hand. "Hey, Josiah. Good to finally meet you. We were calling you River Boy for awhile."

Josiah shook his hand. I could tell he was nervous by the way his smile wobbled. "I'll go by that name, sir."

Jake stood up to introduce himself. "Hey, Josiah." He

and Josiah shook hands. I held my breath. I knew Jake was going to say some wisecrack. "I guess you don't mind those fiery types, huh?"

I glared at my stupid brother and took Josiah into the kitchen. "Here, Ma." I handed her the flowers. "Josiah brought you these." Ma said how pretty they were and got out a little vase. I asked Josiah, "Have you read our ad?"

"I haven't had time to buy a newspaper. What about you?"

"I was waiting for you to get here. I took the newspaper off the porch so my family couldn't look at it either. Are you nervous?"

"I hope they didn't change it or make it sound silly."

"I know. I don't want my family to laugh. But Jake probably will."

Ma cut in. "Jake's humor sometimes gets the better of us all, but I'd be hard pressed to believe that any son of mine would make fun of the courage you both have."

"Courage?" I asked.

Ma placed the violets on the table, which was set with our nice dishes. "I mean when someone says, 'Tell me about you. I want to know,' they're going to hear all of it, the good and the bad."

Her words made me think of my talk with Pa in the barn.

We gathered around the table, Ma and Pa and my brothers and my friend. Caleb said the blessing. We echoed our amens and sat down. We started passing around the food and talking together. I'm sure it was a moment to enjoy, but I couldn't hold off any longer. I ran to the parlor.

"Where's she off to?" I heard Pa ask.

Josiah and Caleb answered at the same time: "Getting the newspaper."

I ran back, turning the pages as fast as I could. "What section will our ad be in?"

"Maybe classifieds," offered Ma.

"What section is that?" I asked.

Pa's voice sounded excited as mine: "Section B. About half way. Section B. You got it?"

I got to the classifieds. Josiah was out of his chair and peering over my shoulder. I held my breath as I looked down the page.

"There it is!" Josiah pointed to a box in the middle of the next page. "There's our ad!" Those were our words. They hadn't even changed a punctuation mark.

"Are you going to read it to us?" asked Ma.

"Here," offered Pa. "Can I read it aloud for everyone?"

I handed Pa the paper. I was scared. What if he read it wrong and everyone laughed?

Pa put on his glasses and cleared his throat.

Our Ad

How do people love and why? The answer is not just for angils and poets. But for me, you, our aunts and unkles and even dogs (or cats or birds, ect). Send us your ideas/stories about love, the letters can be real or in your imaginaton, funny or sad. And not just romantick. You can mail responces to the Lynn Post Office, to Clara Reese and Josiah Fry. Or drop it off there if you dont want to pay postige.

Pa read the words. No one laughed, not even Jake. They did ask lots of questions, like why we were asking for stories about love and what we were going to do with them. Josiah and I had made a pact, though—we weren't telling anyone until our book was done.

I thought they'd keep asking, but after one or two firm no's, they did something that took me by surprise. After dinner, they all went and wrote down their letters. While Josiah and I did the dishes, Pa and Jake sat down on the kitchen table and wrote away. Caleb and Ma went to the living room and wrote their ideas on Ma's pretty stationary. I thought they'd give the papers to us, but Ma collected them all, put them in an envelope and addressed it to the post office.

Josiah and I could barely concentrate on our checkers game. Our book was beginning around us, right now!

Around eight o'clock that night, Pa offered Josiah a ride home.

"No thanks, sir," he answered, helping me store away the checkers. "I'll just walk home."

I walked Josiah to the door. "I'm glad you got to come over."

Josiah didn't say anything as he walked from the porch to the grass.

Then he turned back and called out in a clear voice, "See you tomorrow, Clara."

I waved at him, his silhouette moving through the night air. I wanted to tell him how I was hoping for him, that our book would change things around—a nice dinner wouldn't be so rare for him, soon. But I held on tight to the porch railings and watched him walk out of sight.

Our book had begun. What were other people thinking about our ad?

It Is Also the Question

It was not long before we found out. The grocer asked me if I was doing a project for school. My Sunday school teacher said we wanted to be poets but lacked experience. The blacksmith, Jake told me, wanted to know if sheriffs had put us up to it to scout out the area.

But Josiah and I thought that the less we told others about our book idea, the better. "They might get all lofty," Josiah mused, "if they know their ideas are heading for a book." I agreed. We would just say that curiosity killed the cat, and it will all come out in the wash.

I warned Josiah that at first we may not get a lot of letters. "Stamina is more Lynn's strong point, you know," I told him, "than speed."

We didn't let ourselves check the post office for one week. "I think it'd be better if we let the letters pile up," Josiah said. "Then we could have the fun of organizing them."

We were sitting on our rock, preparing for the letters.

Josiah brought his notebook and started labeling the tops of the pages: "From children." "From adults." "Funny." "Stories." I found an old metal box my Pa used to file his bank papers in. "We can file the letters in here," I told him. "And we can keep them here by the river. Waterproof and secret."

"The river has even more secrets to keep, now." Josiah looked around. "I think this is the best office editors could ask for."

We put the notebook in the box, locked it tight, and snuggled it among the roots of one of the trees on our bank. Everything was ready for the stories that would become our book. The book that would get Josiah and Lydia a better place to live.

At the end of the week, I woke up with butterflies in my tummy. I put on my favorite dress, a blue one with a lace collar, and met Josiah a block from the post office. I noticed his hair was carefully combed.

"Are you ready?" he asked when he saw me.

"I was just about to ask you that," I replied. "And *yes*. I am."

The bell on the post office door jingled as we entered. Mr. Bedford walked in from the back office.

"Good morning, kids."

"Good morning, Mr. Bedford," we answered. I could hear the excitement in Josiah's voice.

Mr. Bedford looked at us. We stood waiting. Something, Pa always said, I wasn't the best at.

"Are there any letters for us, Mr. Bedford? From our ad? That's why we're here," I said.

Mr. Bedford gave a little smirk. "Of course! Let's see here." Mr. Bedford ran his fingers over the tiny slots along the wall behind him.

Huh? Surely there were more letters than that. He pulled out my family's envelope and only two more. I couldn't look at Josiah.

"I see that your ad wasn't so successful," Mr. Bedford said. "So sorry about that."

I looked at him. The man wasn't sorry at all. He probably thought we were wasting everyone's time, especially his.

"Good day," he said.

"Good day," I said in my most fake-sweet tone, and we left his stinking post office.

Out on the sidewalk, we looked at the envelopes. I still couldn't look Josiah in the eye. It seemed best just to press through.

"Let's see. Who are these from?" I picked the top letter up. The penmanship was lovely. "It's from Mrs. Foster! The minister's wife! If we tell some women that she wrote us, we'll be home free. We'll get *too* many letters." I felt better already and tore open the letter with gusto.

"Who's the other letter from?" Josiah took up the second envelope. "There's no return address." He opened it and read the letter. A light came back into his eyes, and it was very bright.

"'Love is the answer,'" Josiah read aloud,

> But it is also the question. Will you come with me? Yes. Will you wait for me? Of course. Will you forget me? No. Whether it is the answer or the question, though, it takes bravery. Love, I think, *is* bravery.

Josiah looked up at me. "Clara, this is what we're looking for."

"Who wrote it?"

Josiah looked at the signature. "Mr. Arthur McNally? Do you know who he is?"

The name sounded familiar. I tried to remember. "Yes—you know who he is too. That's the Heron." The Heron got that name from how, when he was younger, he went south every winter. But he hadn't left Lynn in a long time, and hardly ever came down from his farm in the mountains. A strange girl lived with him, his daughter or his niece, who he took care of. I'd always heard there was something wrong with her, that she never grew up.

"I didn't think of this, Clara, but what might be the most interesting thing is *who* sends a reply. So what did

Mrs. Foster write?" I thought of the lady who sat in the front pew every week, her face both alert and tired, with a bright flower in her plain hat.

I couldn't wait to read it, but as I looked at her letter, I paused to inspect her penmanship. All the loops and lines were so pretty.

"Well?" Josiah prodded.

I read the letter to him:

> Dear Josiah and Clara,
>
> How kind of you to ask for our stories. I have given your advertisement some thought. Here is my answer.
>
> Love is something that we can feel and something that we long for. It's close to us, and yet sometimes it is hard to remember it's there.
>
> It's like when I swam as a child in the big lakes near my house, in Texas. Every once in awhile, my toe touched the floor beneath the waters. A tiny touch, and I knew the ground under me was holding me and all the water in the lake.
>
> It is there whether I am feeling it or not, and I love love for that.
>
> I hope this reply suits your request.
>
> Yours truly,
> Geraldine Foster

I glanced up at Josiah. I didn't get all she said, but I got that she was helping us. "What a lady," I said.

Josiah replied, "It's like we owe her something." I remembered what Ma said about our courage. I thought of the Heron and Mrs. Foster writing to us, picking up a pen and writing. Josiah was thinking too, and we were both looking toward each other, but not at each other. Then, our eyes caught, and we really saw each other.

"Ice cream on me," I said. We started walking away, when Mr. Bedford stuck his head out the door. "So sorry to detain you. But I just found another letter. It's from," he sighed, "my brother's wife."

Poor lady. But I thanked Mr. Bedford all the same.

"Now a little word from Mrs. Bedford," Josiah said as we walked the two blocks to the pharmacy. He unfolded the paper, and we read it together silently. There were scratch outs all over the paper.

> I don't know ~~a lot~~ about love, as in words ~~and the like~~. But I love my Danny very much, and ~~when we don't have kids~~ we are alone, just us. But the quiet with him is not the quiet when I am alone, and ~~talking being~~ talking and being with him is better than conversation with anyone else. He makes living with his family not too bad.

P.S. Danny is my husband. He's way
more fun than the rest of his family!

Josiah folded the letter very carefully and put it with
the others in his satchel.

"You know what I think?" he asked.

"The only thing to top this is ice cream."

"Two scoops, please."

"Me too," I said.

Miss Tilly nodded. Strands of her dark hair gently
bobbed too. "Two scoops it is," she said in her deep,
throaty voice. Since before I was born, Miss Tilly has been
making her ice cream so good most people in Lynn didn't
bother making their own.

"So what brings you two here today?" she asked as
she handed us our treats.

We carefully counted out the coins onto the counter. I
replied, "We're picking up the letters to our ad. At the
post office."

"I saw that ad you put in the paper about love."

"Are you going to write something?" Josiah asked.

Miss Tilly pursed her lips together. "I had given it
some thought. Not that," she added hastily, "I really have
experience   with   romance."   Reputations   were   very
important in our town.

"It doesn't have to be about *romance*, Miss Tilly," Josiah said, taking his ice cream.

"Well, I was just going to put down some things." She paused. "Some *observations* about people that come in here."

Josiah's eyes lit up. "That's a good idea."

Miss Tilly smiled. "Maybe I will. Anyways, right now I've got to wash some dishes." And with that she lifted a wooden box and went to the sink in the back room.

The ice cream was cool and sweet, and even though we only got a few letters, they were really honest ones. The day was turning out to be okay.

That was before Dr. Lowell walked in.

Think of His Grief

A long time ago, Dr. Lowell was a teacher of poetry and stories. He moved to Boston and taught at a college there. When he returned, a woman named Tamsin was with him. She was his bride.

Dr. Lowell then started a printing shop named Quincy Press, and he and Tamsin had a daughter named Sophie. Quincy Press made poem books and college things, but after what happened to his wife and daughter, Dr. Lowell went into the newspaper business. Pa said it was to keep him as busy as possible.

One morning, Tamsin and Sophie were playing by a river, and little Sophie fell into the water. By the time Tamsin found her, it was too late.

The townspeople didn't see much of the teacher and Tamsin after that, and then the next thing happened. Tamsin disappeared. A telegram arrived a week later, and it said that she had to leave our town. Dr. Lowell never printed another poem again—that's when he began his newspaper. Since then, he's run a tight ship at the press.

One night the previous spring, my parents hosted a committee meeting for a new school building. I thought it would be great fun to pretend to be the maid, and with enough begging, Ma let me. I put on my dark navy dress, and a white apron, and did my hair back in braids. When people arrived, I greeted them with a little curtsey and took their hats and coats. Of course everyone knew who I was, but some of the adults were glad to play along as I called them "madam" and "sir." Then, when people were seated in the parlor, I took around a tray with cups of hot cider.

At the start, the meeting was exciting. Some adults were pushing for a brick building with a small library and maybe even a gym. Though it would be a couple years before we'd see such a building, my heart skipped a beat to think of that. I thought I would be good at this game called basketball.

But some adults were arguing the expense wasn't worth it, when a new sturdy wooden building would be just fine.

I passed by Dr. Lowell, holding out a tray of cups. He waved his hand to shoo me away. His eyes were dark as he tugged on his charcoal-gray beard. When there was a pause in the conversation, he spoke in a low, cool, sarcastic tone: "The children of ranchers and miners are hardly scholars. Why pour in money to a school like this?"

Ma asked back, "What do you think would be a better way to spend the money, Dr. Lowell?"

"I would rather see some new roads. At least then we'd know the benefit, and not waste books and bricks on soon-to-be cowhands and soon-to-be miners."

"But, Lowell," a man said, "You wrote books!"

"And I know firsthand how wasteful such an education can be. A simple school building for a simple education is enough for Lynn."

I frowned—surely he thought better of us than that.

"Come, now," another man said. "Think how it will help our children, having such a big, strong building to attend—they might not all want to be cowhands, Lowell."

"Come now!" Dr. Lowell mocked back, as the room grew quiet and cold. "How deep is your head stuck in the sand, that you would think anything good can come out of this small, dusty, worthless town!"

"Worthless? I tell you, if you had a child, you'd think differently!"

The air sizzled. My hands gripped the tray tight, and I was afraid to look at Dr. Lowell.

Dr. Lowell stood slowly, spoke slowly. "If I had a child, I wouldn't build a new school for her. I'd take her away from this ugly little mining town." He started to walk out of the room.

The other man tried to stop him. "Lowell, I wasn't thinking when I spoke—I'm sorry, god-awful sorry—"

"So am I. Well, I can promise you this, my paper won't cover any news on your beloved little school project. Such news isn't worth the ink."

"Oh, now—please don't use the power of the newspaper like that," another man said. Dr. Lowell cast a look of sheer, hateful disgust around the room, and walked out.

The room was deadly quiet. Ma caught my eye and motioned for me to leave the room. I obeyed, heart pumping heavily.

Later that night, I heard Pa say that Dr. Lowell was getting too powerful with that paper of his. "It's a shame for our town that he runs the paper. He's gotten so *cold*, Violet, and so harsh."

Ma said, "But think of his grief, Frank."

So it was with surprise that I saw Dr. Lowell enter Miss Tilly's on a work day. What flavor would he choose?

I gasped as I saw his tall body lean toward us like a greyhound on a trail. He wasn't here for ice cream. He was here for us.

Josiah looked to see what the matter was and turned right into him.

"Are you Josiah Fry and Clara Reese?"

We nodded.

Dr. Lowell's lips tightened into a thin line. "Mr. Bedford told me I might find you here."

Trust Mr. Bedford to rat out kids.

Dr. Lowell looked closely at us. Then he spoke—slowly, like we might not understand him. His voice was cold as a winter wind. "Did you two bring in the advertisement about love?"

We nodded again, this time more slowly.

"Tell me now. What fool of a staff member did you give it to? Who in my office allowed you two poorly educated kids to submit such ill-written, ill-begotten nonsense?"

My mouth dropped open. "He wasn't a fool. He was a very nice man."

"His name?" His voice was sharp.

I opened my mouth to speak but Josiah kicked my leg.

"We don't remember his name," Josiah replied firmly. I didn't think Josiah would talk at all, and here he was being brave. Unfortunately, it made me smile.

"Do you think this is funny, Miss Reese? Do you think it's funny that your silly, stupid advertisement has made my paper a laughing stock? It has the first mistakes in the paper for the past *seven* years!" He bent down lower, and his voice got even colder: "You—think—it's—funny?"

No adult had ever spoken to me in such a scary way. "No, sir," I whispered.

Josiah said, "Dr. Lowell, I'm sorry about the mistakes. I wouldn't have asked them to keep it just as it was, if I knew it mattered so much."

Dr. Lowell was staring at Josiah as if he were trying to recognize who the young boy was.

Josiah continued, "And I don't think it's been a laughing stock. I mean, the pastor's wife responded. And I don't think it's silly. Clara and I are going to use all the responses to make a book." When Josiah said the word *book*, he couldn't help sounding a little proud. I held my breath. What would Dr. Lowell say now?

Dr. Lowell squinted his eyes. "I know who you are. You're Old Fry's son. Look just like your sister." Dr. Lowell paused. "So *you're* writing a book about love? Pardon my ignorance," he began, and the sarcasm in his voice hit us again like a cold winter wind, "But tell me. How is a book about love going to be written by the son of the town drunkard?"

Josiah's face went pale, then red. I stood up, and my anger was so deep that I felt dizzy.

My voice was louder than I expected. "Shut up, you! Everyone will want to read it! It's better than your stodgy, boring old books and poems any day of the week!"

"Dear me. Only Violet Reese could have such an impudent, sassy daughter. Why that redhead mother of yours was so jealous of your father's friendship with Tamsin—"

Josiah bolted up out of his chair. "That is *enough*. You can say what you like about me, I've heard it all before. But don't you dare say anything about Clara's family, don't you *dare*." Josiah's eyes were big with anger, and his cheeks were flushed. He leaned towards me and grabbed my hand. "Come on, Clara, let's get out of here."

We left Dr. Lowell standing by our table, his face in a tight scowl. There was something beneath the scowl, though, some look. It has taken me awhile to know what it was, and why it was so deep in his eyes. I think now that it was a look of shame.

In Vast Ways

A few mornings later, Josiah met me at the rock with two new envelopes.

"One's from Miss Tilly. Open that one first," Josiah said as he handed me the letters. I tore it open and read it aloud.

> I was meaning to write some observations about people, but there is a story I got to tell about why I make my ice cream. I grew up without a ma, and my pa was more often than not out working. He was a logger, which is a kind of work that pulls and pulls on your energy. But there was this one Sunday afternoon where all the churches put on a fair, and Pa was not too tired, so we went.
>
> And wouldn't you know, but there's a wood-chopping contest. Pa beat everyone so bad that they gave him the first and second place prizes: an ice cream maker

and a kite. We was so proud of him, and he knew it and he liked that. And that's how I got so good at making ice cream and a living for myself.

Miss Tilly

The other envelope had no writing on it. I opened it and read it.

Josiah heard me sigh softly. "What? What is it?"

I handed the letter to him. While Josiah read it, the only sound was the sound of our river.

Love is seeing past all you don't like, like the smell of beer and a loud voice, and loving what you don't see, like your brother's dreams. It is the way you know someone is, deep down, when an angel sings or flaps its wings, when God says "Show them," and you see for one tiny, spectacular moment what to love, and why to love. And that's how love, which doesn't really make sense to us at all, if we think about it, that's how it comes together in us, and that's how we can love in vast ways.

Lydia Fry

I watched Josiah's lips mouth the words. He read the

letter three times and after the third time he looked up at me.

"My father ..."

He stopped. I did not know where to look. I wanted to look away. But I also wanted to stop the earth as it spun so that I could know what my friend needed, and I could say it or do it or win it or catch it. I did not know what he needed, so I waited, and his next words filled the river.

"Clara, I have to tell you. There are times when my pa—he yells at me and hits me. He doesn't do it all the time, only when he's real drunk. I don't know—I don't know why."

I didn't know what to say back. I could not think of the right words. I asked, "Can you run away?"

"No. I won't leave my sister."

The water swept around the rock. It was like we were on a raft. I said the words aloud: "It's like we're on a raft when we're on this rock."

How did I know to say that? I do not know, and yet they were the right words. Josiah's eyes took on a strange, sad gladness—maybe he thought this, that he was on the move, moving from a shadowed room to somewhere else, and with a friend. That's when I decided that come hell or high water, this book was going to get Josiah safe.

When It Is a Word

Josiah and I had not yet opened my family's letters. We were originally going to wait for the rush of letters to slow down.

"Since there never was a rush, now's as good a time as any," Josiah said. It was the next day and we were sitting on our rock with the metal box between us.

With a flutter in my stomach, I ripped open the large envelope. Four pieces of paper were neatly folded. I drew them out and handed two to Josiah. We read them in silence.

The first two I had were Jake's and Ma's. Ma's was short.

> Love! I see it in leaf patterns and in the ways the clouds move, the way even voiceless things speak of great tenderness. But when love has a voice, when I hear it in a word, when it is a word, it is glorious.

I read Jake's next, and it was him all over.

Love is like getting a new car and wanting to go everywhere—mountains, sea, city, all over the world—with that one person beside you.

Josiah and I traded letters. I recognized Caleb's handwriting in the first one.

I can't seem to find words for this. It's simple like a song you know real well or feeling safe at home late at night. It's also like swinging from a rope into a rushing river or standing outside when there's thunder and lightning. And you want to stop the world so the person you love has peace and can see herself as true and real and full of meaning.

I wondered how he knew to write that. That's exactly how I felt when Josiah told me about his father.

Then, I opened my own father's letter.

Love came to me through darkness, and sometimes I still distrust it. But this is what comes to my mind, Clara and Josiah. Love is . . . it's an old man giving his dog, his only friend, to someone else, because he can no longer afford to feed it.

It was quiet. Then Josiah spoke: "We've got to get more letters, Clara. We've got to make our book. I want everyone to read these."

So we decided to go into town and thank Miss Tilly for her letter. Then we could ask her to spread the word to each and every person that came to buy her ice cream. We had no idea the rumble that was ahead.

The Rumble in Town

The bell jingled as we walked into Miss Tilly's. Quick as a heartbeat, Miss Tilly was before us. She was frantic. "Oh, my dears, my dears, my dears. That dreadful man, that dreadful, dreadful man!"

We stared at her. I found my voice. "What in Sam Hill are you talking about, Miss Tilly?"

She stopped mid-word and her mouth formed a giant O. Miss Tilly walked quickly over to the counter and reached behind it to grab a newspaper. She handed it to us.

It took a second to find what was so bad. I think Josiah and I saw the words at the same time. The letters were sharp as daggers.

> Dear Readers of *The Lynn Coaster*: Please pardon the errors in an advertisement that came out in the paper for Sunday, July 23, which asked for your stories. Unfortunately, the staff

was unaware that children were posting this advertisement, and now that the full situation has come to our attention, we ask that you please ignore the request and forgive the paper its foolishness.

Dr. Lowell, Editor-in-Chief

We looked at each other. This was about *our* ad?

Miss Tilly stopped wringing her hands. "I couldn't believe my eyes. I thought you two had already seen it."

"Our family only gets the paper on Sunday," I mumbled. I was trying to make sense of Dr. Lowell's notice. Why was he being so mean? Why did he call it foolishness? That big-head idiot had no idea that this book was Josiah's way out.

At that moment, two things happened. Caleb was at the door, and the big black phone in the back of the pharmacy rang. Miss Tilly ran to the phone as I swung open the door.

"Did you hear?" I asked Caleb. I could tell he had—his eyes were filled with anger.

"I was dropping feed off at Mr. Johnson's, and his wife came out and showed me Lowell's notice. She thought this little town feud was actually funny."

Miss Tilly called from the back. "Josiah! Your sister Lydia's on the phone!"

Josiah ran to the phone. I looked up at Caleb, and I saw a flicker of something, a look that crossed his face when he heard the name Lydia. It was like light on water. Suddenly, the way he talked about Lydia to Ma and Pa, and his letter too, made sense. Jacob was not the only one who had liked Josiah's sister.

Josiah came running back. "Lydia's just read the ad at work and has been trying to find me." He shook his head. "She wants us to come by. Boy, she's angry."

A little anger is just what we needed. We'd somehow fight for these stories. For our book.

As we ran out, I grabbed Caleb's hand. "Don't think you're staying behind!"

"Don't think I was planning to!"

Our Next Move

"So what are you going to do?" Lydia asked us.

We had just walked into the bank where she worked at a side desk. I was watching her closely to see how she would react when she saw Caleb. I wasn't let down. When she saw him, she smoothed her hair and straightened her soft-blue dress.

So it was Caleb, not Jake, she liked. Was that why Caleb pretended not to like her? These grown-ups were too confusing to follow.

Before we replied, she turned to Caleb. "I don't get why he printed something so mean."

Caleb was running his hand through his hair. "I was really surprised too. I think the ad embarrassed him."

Josiah asked, "You mean, he thinks his readers are laughing at him?"

"It was unusual."

Lydia agreed, "It was strange—but that's what was good about it. You've got to finish what you started. You asked people to be bold, now you got to be."

"So what's our next move?" I asked Josiah.

He must have been ready for that question because he spoke without the time it takes to think: "We're going to put signs around town. And we're going to keep asking people for their stories, and we're going to make this book, and it won't be foolishness."

A man from a nearby desk came over. I had seen him at some town meetings. I think his name was Mr. Coleman.

"Are you the kids who put in that ad in Lowell's paper?"

"Yes, sir," I said.

"I couldn't help overhearing your plans. I feel I must say something." He cleared his throat, and Caleb and Lydia glanced at each other. "Dr. Lowell has a point. Many people outside of Lynn order our newspaper because they can trust its accuracy and prestige. Don't do anything to hurt the paper." He was so serious that there were three creases in between his eyebrows.

Caleb stopped wringing his hat, and Lydia looked downright angry. A million words came to my mind, but it was Josiah who spoke. "What good is a paper, sir, if it can't ask for stories from its readers?"

Mr. Coleman gave a stiff shrug before walking away. But he had given me an idea. The word *prestige* sent a picture into my mind of a lady with white gloves. I turned to Josiah and said, "Before we hang up the signs, I think we better do something. Meet me at the town square as fast as you can with your best clothes on!"

We ran out of the bank. It wasn't until I was almost home that I realized Caleb hadn't moved from his spot by Lydia's desk.

Half an hour later we were walking up Lorraine Street, which has lovely wooden houses with roses. I still hadn't told Josiah where we were headed, because I didn't want him turning back.

"You won't even give me a hint?" he asked.

We arrived at 42 Lorraine Street, and I nodded to the house. "Here we are. Follow me."

I marched up the walkway and knocked on the door. Through the window, I saw a figure coming toward us. I heard Josiah gasp.

"You brought us *here*?" He looked ready to bolt, but the door swung open before he could move.

Mrs. Foster, the pastor's wife, stood before us. I could tell by her look that she had already read the paper. "Clara. Josiah. Tell me how I can help."

Josiah's heart was won. Mrs. Foster brought us inside her house and served us tea in her parlor, which was very cozy and had green velvet chairs. She even used fancy cups and saucers, but I was too nervous about breaking the darn things to enjoy them.

"So, the man at the bank gave me an idea," I said.

"Would it be all right," I asked Mrs. Foster, looking at her directly, "If we copied your letter onto our signs?"

She looked at me with great thoughtfulness. I held my breath, and Josiah did too. Then she said these words: "I'm going to be honest with you. The thought of everyone seeing those words is scary. But I have to tell you, it's exciting too. Use my letter."

We stood up, and Mrs. Foster followed us to the door. Josiah must have got another idea on the way out, because instead of walking over the threshold, he leapt over it. "Mrs. Foster, do you know where the Heron lives? Mr. Arthur McNally?"

"I think he lives up by Turtle Creek. Up on Boar's Hill."

Josiah told Mrs. Foster, "It won't just be your story on those signs, ma'am. We'll get you some company." I got what Josiah was thinking. We'd ask the Heron if we could put his letter on our signs too.

Lilac and the Heron

The path to Boar's Hill was long and overgrown. I had been to Turtle Creek once with Jake to go fishing, but that had been a couple before.

"Nobody has been on this path for a long time," Josiah said. "Does the Heron go into town at all?"

We heard the sound of the creek and followed it until a house came into view. I didn't see the Heron anywhere. Josiah and I started whistling so that the Heron could hear that company was coming. Then, I heard someone singing. I looked around and saw an older girl in a small garden. She was pulling weeds, I think. I wondered if she were the strange girl I had heard about. When she saw us, she crouched behind some tall plants.

"Should we stay?" I asked.

"I don't know. I hope he doesn't think that we're just trespassing."

Then, we saw the Heron walking toward us from the woods. He had a long brown beard and wide shoulders and was carrying a big canvas bag. He called out a strange greeting: "Peace and salutations!" He must have guessed who we were because he said, "I'm thinking you're the ones I sent the letter to!" He walked toward us.

"Yes, sir," I said. I tried out his greeting. "Peace and salutations." He looked over at me and smiled.

Josiah told him, "You won't believe what's happened in town today, sir, but there's a notice in the paper asking people to ignore our ad. We were wondering if you could help us."

The Heron swung his bag down to the porch. "But what can I do?"

"We want to put signs around town, telling people we're still looking for the stories. Could we copy your letter onto some?"

"Do you think others would care about my letter?"

"Yes. I know you don't come into town much, but people respect you, 'specially since you take care of . . ." Josiah glanced towards the girl in the garden. "Is she your daughter? Clara and I don't know."

The Heron's eyes softened. "That's Lilac. She's my niece. Her mother was my older sister."

"What was your sister's name?" Josiah asked.

The Heron sat on the steps of the porch. "Rose. She was ten years older than me. She was like my mother. You see, she died when I was fourteen, and I promised her I'd take care of Lilac."

"How old is Lilac now?"

The Heron grinned at Josiah. "You sure like your stories. Lilac's an adult now, but she's still child-like, in her own way." He glanced at her and then back at us. "She's a little shy, but if you come again, she'll recognize you and maybe she'll come over and say hello."

I thought how this book idea was bringing us into the lives of others. Josiah and I would have never come to Turtle Creek or known the story of Lilac.

The Heron spoke. "If my letter can help you, use it."

Before we left, the Heron gave us some beef jerky, seeds for our garden, interesting fishing hooks, and even a few tips for trout-fishing in the creeks of Buntain. Josiah and I walked away waving to the Heron. Lilac waved to us too.

We hurried down the overgrown path, anxious to make our signs. That big cheese Dr. Lowell had no idea who he'd messed with.

The Way for Others

By the time we made it back to my house, it was early afternoon. Ma came out to meet us. I could tell she was angry because her face was red and her lips were tight, but she was also trying to watch her words because all she said was, "That blasted man!"

We told her how Mrs. Foster and the Heron were letting us use their letters for the signs, and Ma said, "So one story will open the way for the others."

We found paper and ink and pens, and made ten signs. On two of them, we wrote our ad. On four of them, I copied Mrs. Foster's letter (I tried to write like her, with all those graceful loops), and on the other four, Josiah copied the Heron's letter.

Josiah saw mine and whistled through his teeth, "Whoo-ee, that's sure going to impress folks."

I looked at his. "Perfectly respectable."

Just as we were going to leave, there came a knock at our front door. I ran and opened it—there stood Lucy, Meredith, Jackson, and Peter. Lucy said, "We read what that mean Dr. Lowell wrote. What can we do to help?"

Josiah and I smiled at each other.

"You could help us make more signs," I said. "And help us hang them up."

Together we went to the kitchen table, and copied more signs. Meredith and Lucy tried to write fancy, too. Lucy did okay, but Meredith's signs looked like a three year old was trying out cursive for the first time. But who cared? Meredith was writing them in kindness, and people might stop and read it just to see what such crazy writing was saying.

Jackson and Peter made a map of the town, and helped plan out where we would post the signs. I served them all lemonade and some of my homemade gingersnaps. Peter ate more of those than I had ever seen anyone eat in one go.

We parted ways and went to hang up our signs. I could tell Josiah was still shy, but the way his eyes shone when he waved goodbye to them made my heart feel kind of funny-glad. I think he liked having friends.

We left with the signs safe in my satchel. The sun was warm and strong.

Miss Tilly liked our signs a lot, and she hung some up in her ice cream parlor. We still had six signs, but I wasn't going to ask that snarky Mr. Bedford.

Pastor Foster was surprised to see his own wife's letter. He actually read it a few times before he gave it back to us. He told us that we were welcome to hang it up anywhere on the outside of the church, along with Mr. MacNally's. The grocer also let us put up two, though we had to buy something from his store.

We thought we better not put one on the front door of the bank because we didn't want to get Mr. Coleman riled up. But Lydia could put one on her desk, so Josiah ran one to her. Finally, we decided to hang up the last one on the side of the road as you entered the town. Now, we would just have to wait and see what these signs and stories would do.

Two days later, Josiah and I walked through town to inspect our signs. What we found shocked us. Except for the sign on Lydia's desk, *they were all gone.* Josiah and I were so angry we didn't know what to say to each other. We didn't know what to do.

What we ended up doing was walking down to our river. We started throwing stones as hard as we could into the water. I pretended the water was Dr. Lowell's messy-haired head. How was I going to help Josiah find a better place to live, if that man met us at every corner?

I was angry, and I knew Josiah was too. But I didn't know how sad he was. It's hurts me to think back how good of friends we were, but how much we still weren't saying. Especially about his pa.

A Dark Morning

I don't know how I woke up and knew. Maybe it was my imagination. Maybe it was what I dreamt just before waking. Maybe it was how the east, where the sky usually lit up the morning like a lantern in a far away house, was still gray and dark. When I pulled back my red curtains I couldn't see the sun. I could barely see the corner of my river. It was Josiah's river too. And I don't know how, but I knew he was there. So I went.

Between the trees, I saw Josiah. Between the brambles and low branches, I could see that he was sitting, not on a rock in the water, but on a fallen log. The metal box was on his lap. I could see that. But leaves were hiding Josiah's face.

When I came to the riverbank, Josiah looked up at me. That's when I saw his face. It was bruised. There was a black mark around his cheek, and his top lip was puffy. What my face looked like, I can only guess from what Josiah did. He jumped up. "Don't look at me like that! I'm not that hurt!"

"Is Lydia all right?" I whispered. We stood facing each other. Seeing his face took something right out of me.

"That's why it happened. He would have never done this if she was there. Her friend was having a baby and she was helping."

"Josiah, your face looks real bad. We got to get someone to help."

A scowl went across his face. He turned back to the fallen tree and picked up the metal box again. Then he said quiet-like, "I can't, Clara. I don't know what they'd do to my pa."

I scowled back at him. "Who cares what happens to your pa, Josiah!"

His head lifted quickly. "You don't know a thing about my pa! I wouldn't ever get him in trouble."

"But he hurt you!"

"What do you know about getting hurt?"

"I know by looking at your face!" I shouted the words, but there were tears all over my face.

"Why are *you* crying?" he shouted back, and his face got tears too. "What do you have to cry about? Your family wrote letters and your ma made us dinner and you don't have to ask people to write about love to *know* about it. Why are *you* crying? Why?" Then, he lifted the box high over his head and threw it into the river like it was his hurt.

"Josiah!" I screamed. His chances of getting away

from that horrible man were going down the river. I ran right into the moving water, trying to grab at the box. But it was flowing fast, going like a toy ship down the creek. I screamed again and went after it still.

Josiah shouted something, but I didn't hear it. The water rose to my waist, going so fast my feet were barely touching the river bed. And then all of the sudden, my feet weren't touching anything but water, and I was caught in a such rush of a current I couldn't steer myself. I could see the metal box in front of me. The box and I were going too fast. The bigger part of the river was coming up.

Josiah's arm swung out and he grabbed hold of me, drawing me close to the shrubby tree he was clinging to. He held me tight but it took me awhile to know I wasn't going downstream anymore. I clasped hold of the thin, rough tree.

"The box!" I whispered. I couldn't believe it. The book was down the river, drowning.

Pulling ourselves up, we climbed onto the bank of the river. Josiah looked right at me, his big bruise close to my face.

"Clara. *Clara*, I'm sorry."

I looked back at him. Oh Josiah, why did you throw away the book? Why are you protecting your pa? Why is it so hard to help you?

I said, "I won't tell on your pa. But you can't stay there any more. You just can't."

He breathed out slow. "I know. I got to talk to my sister. We got to find another place to stay. But she can't afford no place of our own, and where can Pa go if we stayed in our place?"

I didn't have any more answers.

The Mail Bag

Over the next couple days, Josiah's face started healing. When Lydia found out what happened, she took herself and Josiah to an inn. They didn't have enough money, but the innkeeper was letting Lydia stay there for a week if Lydia did the laundry. Josiah asked me not to tell anyone. Lydia was as proud as him, so I said I'd keep quiet.

But that plan was only good for a week. And our book was at the bottom of the river. And Dr. Lowell had taken down our signs. I was so angry that Caleb took pity and gave me some extra money for ice cream. I was going to go grab Josiah and head over to Miss Tilly's, when I got a bright-red idea. It was bright-red *hot*.

I went to Miss Tilly's on my own. I told her my idea, and her face made that giant O all over again. But I could tell she liked it. She told me, "Girl, you've got gumption."

"Miss Tilly, that's not it. That's not it at all. I've got a friend who needs help."

For the next week or so, Josiah and I tried our best to return to how it was, when we were having such fun together. But the gingersnaps weren't so tasty, and Josiah's stories were always sad. Celeste the star got lost on her way back to star-country and kept asking the moon, "Which way now?"

I hoped Miss Tilly had carried out my plan. That's all I was holding onto.

It was Saturday morning. I was sitting on my braided rug, dolls in front of me. Boy, they were boring the tears out of me. A knock on my door—I looked up.

"Jake the Snake," I said.

"I got something for you."

"Oh, yeah? Finally getting rid of your man's perfume?"

"Do you want your message or not? It's from Miss Tilly."

I froze. "Tell me."

"Last night on the way to the tavern, I saw her closing up. She said to tell you, 'It's happened, they're here.' What, Clar-o, does *that* mean?"

I stood up slowly. "What else did Miss Tilly say, Jake?"

"That all. 'It's happened. They're here.'"

I didn't know if Jake would ever be a messenger for me again—I screamed my head off and ran downstairs. I didn't stop until I was at Josiah's house, and the two of us were on our way to town.

"But why?" Josiah asked again, gasping for air as we neared Main Street. "What's going on?"

"Just you wait," I said.

The bell announced us at Miss Tilly's. Miss Tilly's eyes widened, and she scurried away to the back room. Josiah looked at me, his eyes as big as question marks.

The bell sounded again, behind us. We turned around. Miss Tilly was standing at the door. "I think you better come out here, kids."

We followed her outside. My heart was beating fast.

Miss Tilly waved her hands, like the magician did at the start of the summer, and stepped aside. Behind her was a mailbag, standing three feet tall and brimming over with mail.

Josiah gasped. I shouted. We ran over to the bag and saw inside letters and letters and letters. We started shouting and jumping in the air. I lifted my face to the sky and tried out a rowdy, three-octave yodel. I had no idea what I was doing, but if ever there was a time to try, it was now.

I spun around to Miss Tilly. "You did it! We did it!"

"All week they've been coming. They've just been coming in."

"Look, Josiah! Everyone has written us! Mr. and Mrs.

Johnson—here's one from Pastor Foster—from girls at my school—even from Mr. Bedford!" Every envelope I took out, I threw into the air to catch again.

Josiah dug further in the bag and brought out another letter. He read it and got real still. "Clara, this one's from Idaho."

I got real still too. "I know. I mean, that doesn't surprise me."

"Huh?"

I looked to Miss Tilly to explain. "Clara asked me to send your ad to *The Helena Weekly*, Josiah. Looks like they got it. And printed it. And people read it. And wrote to you."

Josiah's eyes got real full. He looked at me.

"This is what we've been waiting for, Josiah. People are writing us their stories. And *we're* going to write the best book in the world."

"I think," Josiah said, "That we are going to need a much bigger box to file these in."

And we carried the bag home between us, singing "From the Land of the Sky-Blue Water" on the way.

More Letters

When we arrived to my house, Ma saw the bag of letters and nearly did a jig. She told Josiah to get himself and Lydia over that night, because she was making a celebration feast.

Josiah and I took the bag out to the back porch with an old trunk Jake got us from the attic.

"I think we should organize them all and then read them," Josiah said. I was dying to read what some girls from my school wrote, but his idea sounded good. We made piles: from Lynn, from Helena, from other cities in Montana, and from places beyond Montana. The soft noise of paper swished in the air as we sorted out the letters in quiet.

When I saw that one was from Lucy, I had to read it:

I know a girl who liked her friend so much
she proved it by stepping in horse poop!
Her friend stepped in it too. And they ain't
even courting!

A little while later, I couldn't believe what I saw. A letter from that bully-brother of hers, Presley. I opened that one, too.

> I think Clara Reese and Josiah Fry are downright crazy. But I guess part of me don't think that. Part of me wishes I had a friend who'd throw green apples at anyone who came after me, when I was running with a limp, because I was so stupid as to have a pail stuck on my foot.

Well, I'd never read anything that was so rude and so kind all at once.

There was even a letter from the newspaper man, Mr. Bertie Jameson:

> Finding love is kind of like finding a story—you hear a rumor, or get a start of an idea, and then you work and research and hunt out facts and put in long hours and suddenly the story becomes its own thing—way bigger than you first imagined, bigger than anything you could call your own—more exciting and detailed all around. I've got a girl back home, Lillian, and boy, she's a story I would research a lifetime. She's got wild, frizzy hair and big

hands and feet, and she tells the best jokes
I ever heard.

Soon after that letter, I got to an envelope with no
writing on it. I opened it to see where it was from, and
inside was a little scrap of paper folded in half.

On the outside of the paper, in big letters, was the
name,

LILAC

"Josiah," I whispered, and together we looked at the
letter in my hand. I unfolded it. Again in big, scraggly
letters, was

THE HERON LOVES ME

Next to it was a picture of a flower.

I held the piece of paper in front of me. It's what it
was all about. Josiah's best book in the world idea. Love
and loving in ways that were vast, like Lydia wrote. Like
Josiah was looking for, like Caleb kept secret in his heart,
like Lilac knew. Like Josiah's mother wrote on her note.

I sat upon the rock thinking of all the faces of all the
people who had sent us these letters, and they seemed so
many and the list came so fast and full and long—it was

like the river. Even when it made no sense, even when it was tough to do. Love was the best and most ancient thing of all.

The sunset was beginning. The sun was high enough to be seen fully, but the horizon was gathering all sorts of colors—pinks, magentas, and oranges. All the colors were opal-like, still very light. In about ten minutes, I thought, all the colors would be thick and rich, and the sun would be half gone.

Josiah and I were finishing up sorting the letters. I looked down, and the last one in my stack was from Mr. Jim Fry. I gave it to Josiah.

Josiah held it in his hands before opening it. He opened it, and read it, and held it in his hands again. Then he handed it to me.

I don't know what to write. But to say I'm proud of him.

Josiah and I looked at each other. I carefully folded the letter back into the envelope and put it in the stack, From Family.

A Harsh, Wild Light

About three weeks later, at the end of August, Josiah and I were sitting at the table in my parlor. A strange and wonderful device called a typewriter was between us. Ma and Pa had found us one to borrow so that we could type all the letters we got.

We had received eighty-seven letters so far. My job was to type the letters, just as they were, and then Josiah would write little comments for each of them. We were grouping them together, so it would be like chapters. Josiah would also write something for each chapter. We were still trying to come up with the title for this book.

One mid-morning, I couldn't help but let a sigh escape from my lips.

"What's the matter, Clara?" Josiah asked.

I shook my head. I was tired of this parlor room—but how I was aching to get this book under way.

"Want to go to Buntain?" Josiah asked.

I looked up. A mid-day break wouldn't slow down the process too much. "You bet I do!"

We packed a swell lunch this time and headed toward the mountain.

Summer had almost passed since our last visit, and the rains had not come so often. The greens had softened to a pale shade, and the dusty trees looked older under the August sunshine.

We rounded the curve, like last time, expecting to see the vista open wide with the strange beauty of burnt trees and fireweed.

The beauty was there all right, but that's not what we saw first. We saw Dr. Lowell, sitting on a log. It looked like he was carving something.

He looked up when he heard us. "Of course you two would be here on my one day off."

Dr. Lowell wasn't going to make me back off from Buntain. I set my satchel down and walked a few paces. I surveyed the surroundings and didn't pay attention at all to the mean man ruining my view.

Dr. Lowell glanced at the two of us. "I saw your ad in *Helena Weekly*."

"Yes, sir," I replied, lifting my chin high. "Eighty-seven responses so far."

"Well done, Miss Reese. But, of course, you might not know—that silly newspaper panders to politics and popularity. I'm sure you can guess what *I* use the *Helena Weekly* for."

A clean, hot sweep of anger filled me. Was this man

actually saying that he wiped his bottom clean with the newspaper that had made our ad so successful? That had helped us—helped Josiah? I was so angry, I was afraid that I would start crying—and I would *not* let this man see me cry.

I spun around and ran down the path. I heard Josiah follow me.

We were halfway down the mountain, when I realized I left my satchel and our lunch. We crept back.

There was the satchel—about ten yards from the log where Dr. Lowell had been sitting. But now he was out further, walking slowly among the fireweeds and burnt forest remains. He was facing away from us. Josiah tiptoed forward.

A strange, weird noise hit our ears. It was a deep, painful, ugly sob—a kind of noise that would hurt your throat coming out. Josiah and I looked at each other, eyes wide.

Dr. Lowell was kneeling down, like crumpled over, right where he was. Even from this distance I could see how tightly fisted his hands were.

Josiah swiftly grabbed the satchel—and we both scrambled down the path as fast as we could. We looked at each other again but didn't say a word. I don't think either of us had ever heard a man make a sound like that before.

We ate our lunch under the big maple tree at the

bottom of Buntain. We discussed names for our book. We spoke softly. Then we hiked home and got to work again.

That week, everyone in town was asking us what was going to happen. Josiah and I were trying to figure that out too. All I knew was that at that point, I would have happily typed into the night if Ma let me. This book was going to help Josiah get a better home.

"Mrs. Foster was telling Ma that if we still wanted to publish our book, we could try writing to a publisher in Helena," I said to Josiah.

"I don't know. I keep thinking about Dr. Lowell. His notice in the paper. That—*noise* he made, Clara. He's missing everything."

The name of that man still made me want to spit. But I sighed and asked, "You want to go visit him?"

"I want to let him read our book."

Later that week, after a whole lot of typing (which Ma and Pa and even Jake helped me do), we were walking to Dr. Lowell's house on Lamb's Crossing. I was carrying our book in my satchel.

When we left my house, the sky above us was yellow and heavy and about to break. A gold light fell on our skin. We turned from the long road to Main Street. And then, from out of this gold light, the rain came. My satchel would keep the book safe, so we kept going. We reveled in the strange rainfall.

Lamb's Crossing was an old path with old houses few and far between. Dr. Lowell's was the first one, a big blue house with a large veranda. As we walked up the path to his house, the rain slowed, the wind stilled, and the sunlight became very bright. It hit my eye like flint; it was a harsh, wild light from behind the clouds, almost too bright to keep my eyes opened.

"Clara," Josiah burst out, "We don't need shelter from the rain, but from the sun!"

We walked up to Dr. Lowell's porch. He opened the door before we knocked.

Josiah spoke. "Dr. Lowell, we've brought you a copy of our book and it's not to show you what we've done in spite of you. We didn't do it in spite of you. And it's not to heap coals of fire on your head by being kind. My sister has one of your old poems 'The Beaver's Edge,' and I've always liked it. I thought you might like this book, and that's why we're letting you borrow it. It's our only copy, so treat it well."

I didn't know Josiah had that speech prepared. Dr. Lowell seemed surprised too. I pulled the book out and held it up to him. He looked confused. He said, so timid I would never think it came from him, "I took down your signs."

I wanted to throw the book right at his face, but Josiah nodded. "I know." He looked up at Dr. Lowell with a glint in his eye. "Who else would have?"

Dr. Lowell stared at him. Then, he held out his hand to take the book.

He walked back into his house, but he didn't close the door. "There's some hot water on the stove if you want tea." He looked back at our wet clothes. "And don't sit down anywhere."

We followed him in. He perched on the edge of a settee, turning the first page. I don't think either of us expected him to read it right away. I hoped I hadn't made too many mistakes typing, because mistakes really seemed to bother that man. We walked into his kitchen, and I found some tea and made us each a cup. We stood in the kitchen while he read. It was very strange.

We heard a sharp intake of breath. He called us in and thrust a page in front of us. "Who wrote this one?"

We read the entry.

> I handled love like it was a burden. But when it was gone, I learned that it had been helping me carry my burdens. I did not figure this out until it was too late.

Josiah answered, "That one came from some town up north. There wasn't any name on it."

Dr. Lowell's face had no mask. "Whoever wrote it— whoever wrote this—" He couldn't finish. He leaned his face into his hands.

I didn't know what to do, but Josiah did. He simply stood there.

After awhile, Dr. Lowell lifted his head. He asked me an odd question: "When were you born?"

"1900, sir."

"Sophie was born three years before that. Maybe she'd be a little taller than you." Then he stood up and seemed to measure how tall that was. He didn't sigh or cry, he just said, "Since she left I haven't printed anything but that newspaper. I'll do it, that is, if you'll let me."

Josiah's face widened in surprise. "What?"

I could barely believe it. Was this it? Was this Josiah's freedom? I could barely form the words, could barely ask the question, "You'll publish our book?"

"Yes."

Unmoving

It was the night before our first big meeting with Dr. Lowell. The night itself started out swell. Caleb, gumption finally equal to the task, asked Lydia out on a date. Josiah and I had no end of talking about it—or at least, I talked about it, wondering where he was going to take her and what she was going to wear. What were they talking about? Were they laughing or being serious?

Josiah joined our family for dinner, and I think he would have stayed later but I just couldn't stop talking about the date. Just when I got to asking if they would get ice cream, and what ice cream, and what Miss Tilly would think—Josiah said, "I'm outta' here. I got to get some sleep before seeing Dr. Lowell tomorrow."

Pa replied, "But don't you want to figure out how Lydia fixed her hair?"

I glared at Pa and walked Josiah to the door. "See you tomorrow," he said, in a low, thrilled voice. I nodded. Tomorrow was the big day for our book.

I went back into the house, settled back by the hearth

with my cocoa, and asked where everyone thought Caleb and Lydia were now.

Jake, Ma, and Pa all shook their heads.

"You bunch of bores," I replied. Settling back into my chair, I daydreamed of the date. Then I thought about the next day when Josiah and I were going to talk about our book. What about those letters that had been lost in the river? Ma was doing needlepoint and Pa was reading and Jake was flipping through a mechanics book. They had no idea how nervous I got just sitting there beside them. How would it all work out for Josiah?

At breakfast I was going to ask Caleb all about last night. But he wasn't there. I asked Ma where he was. She shook her head, puzzled. "I guess he got an early start. The market's next week. I know we needed some supplies." I ate my eggs and toast lickety-split. Maybe Josiah had heard from Lydia how their night on the town had been.

I was waiting by the river. Josiah was late. I wonder if, deep down, I knew something was wrong. Maybe that's why in my gut I was starting to panic, even though my friend was only a few minutes late.

I heard rustling. Turned south. It was Lydia.

My mouth suddenly tasted bad.

She stopped five feet away. Her face said everything. It

was angry and sad, swollen with tears.

"Oh my God," I whispered. "What happened?"

"I came home last night—he, had, fallen back. Hit his head on the corner of our table. My Pa—was trying to wake him up. Caleb took us to the hotel. Got the doctor. But the doctor needs help. Caleb left last night, or maybe it was this morning. He went to Virginia City for the doctor there."

I looked right at her. I felt cold and angry and wasn't going to hide it. "Fallen back? Your pa hit him!"

She looked right at me. "I know," she whispered.

"Can I see him?" I asked.

"In a couple of hours. No one's allowed but the doctor and nurse."

"He's not awake?"

"He woke up for a few minutes this morning. He—he said your name."

Such a big weight hit my chest it could have been a boulder from the river. I leaned over, gasping, trying to exhale. I looked up to Lydia. "You're not going back there."

She breathed in quick. "I know. Oh God, Clara—" and she lifted her head, and looked up to the trees, and I saw the panic and fear. Where would she go then? How could she support her brother?

I knew what I had to do. I hugged her, and she hugged me, and I made my way to Dr. Lowell's.

I had not noticed before, but Dr. Lowell's porch was filled with ferns. There must have been twenty of them, all different shapes and sizes. I was looking at them as I heard his footsteps come to answer the knock on his door.

"You're early," he said through the screen door.

"Josiah got real ill. I know it's not professional. But he was *really* looking forward to the meeting today. He can't wait—" I heard my voice shake and swallowed. I said, more clearly, "He can't wait to meet with you, Dr. Lowell."

His face was stern. "Is he all right?"

I swallowed again. I couldn't get a word past my throat. I shrugged.

"I've made a few corrections in the book. Shall I wait to go over them with Josiah, or talk with you?"

"Oh—" I thought about it. "Wait for Josiah. He likes stuff like that."

"Not your cup of tea?"

I made a face. "I'd rather be fishing."

Dr. Lowell actually grinned and asked, "Would you like to join me for a real cup of tea?"

The pain I felt squeezed really hard, right in my ribs. "No," I gasped. "I've got to get back to Josiah."

Another stern look passed across the man's face. "Clara? Are *you* all right?"

"Oh, Dr. Lowell, answer me quick. If this book does

really well, it will give Josiah some money, right? How much will it bring him? How fast can he get it?"

Dr. Lowell looked right at me. "Did Josiah do this for money?"

"No, he's never said anything like that. It's me. It's me that's asking. I want Josiah to get loads of money. It's the only way—to leave—his father—" As I said the words that I had never told anyone, my great hopes for the book, I could not keep the tears from my eyes.

Dr. Lowell knelt down. "Clara. Books—don't make that much—and it would be, a long time yet—"

A spasm of pain made me tremble. "But that's his only way out!"

Dr. Lowell's eyes got wider. He whispered in a tone I didn't know was in him, "My dear girl."

Ma was sitting next to me in the hotel lobby, but it seemed she was across the room. I looked at my hands on my lap. They seemed bigger than usual. I glanced across the room. Caleb and Lydia were sitting on a horse-hair settee right underneath the one window in the room. The window was dingy and stained with old raindrops. Why hadn't they cleaned it? Stupid hotel.

The doctor from Virginia City was coming down the stairs. Our doctor, Dr. Wilson, was right behind him. We all stood up.

The strange doctor said some words I didn't

understand. I only got what he said at the end: "We now just have to wait for the boy to wake up."

Ma's face was taut, scared. I had never seen that face. I didn't know what to do. I buried my face into that place just above her waist. I let some crying out. But I couldn't get it all out. It was lodged somewhere, below where crying comes from.

That hollow feeling I had at the start of summer—before I met Josiah, what Josiah took away—was back. But it was different. It hurt now, hurt bad.

I was sitting next to Josiah, reading some of Dr. Lowell's poems like "The Beaver's Edge." Josiah was lying there, unmoving, eyes shut.

I heard someone out in the hallway, trying to walk real quiet. I walked over to the door.

It was Lucy and Jackson out there. Their faces were dim in the hallway, and I could tell they were a little scared.

"Hey, Lucy," I said. "Hey, Jackson."

Lucy whispered, "We heard about Josiah, Clara. We wanted to come by—not to bother you none. Just to say we're thinking about you."

I nodded. That place where crying comes from was burning bad. "Thanks, you two. Thanks so much."

"You keep us posted," Jackson said. "You tell us anything we can help with, okay?"

"You got it."

I went back into the room. I sat back down. I leaned in toward Josiah. "Our friends were here," I told him. "Your friends. They're asking about you, Josiah."

About an hour went by. A nurse walked in. She said, "A man's here to see Josiah." I nodded. Dr. Lowell must have heard the news.

But it wasn't Dr. Lowell. It was someone I had never met before, but I knew right away who he was. It was Old Man Fry. He walked up to the doorway, his face bowed low. I stood up, feeling a little dizzy. Was that anger or fear I was feeling?

The man shuffled in from the dark hallway. He lifted his face, but he didn't see me. He was looking right at Josiah. The look of despair on his face was so deep that I swayed back. Before any word could be said by the nurse or me, he turned away, limping badly.

I sat back down. Gingerly I touched Josiah's hand. "Josiah?" I asked. "River Boy! You've got to wake up. Your pa's worried something awful. And we've got to work on your book. Dr. Lowell has some interesting corrections."

But his eyes stayed closed.

Ma returned to the hotel with supper for Lydia, Caleb, and me. After we had eaten, Ma quietly asked if I would come home. "You can sleep, Clara, and be back tomorrow."

I looked at her. I felt so tired. Home sounded like a good idea. "Okay."

At home, Pa and Jake each gave me a hug. Ma gave me a small cup of warm milk, and then I went upstairs to bed. I thought of all the lovely things around me—the bright dandelion quilt on my bed, the cup of warm milk, the kind men in my family, the lanterns with clean glass, the way Ma had stewed apples for our dinner. Then I thought again of those curtains Lydia had sewn and hung and the small cup of flowers on their table. They too were pieces of love and care, but they weren't strong enough. They hadn't protected my friend. I hadn't either.

Here

"Clara, you don't have to stay here. Not all day." Lydia spoke from across the hotel room. Her eyes seemed sunk in, like she wasn't sleeping at all. "You've got to get outside and get some of that summer sunshine."

"I don't want summer sunshine. Summer sunshine makes me sick," I said. I said it in a harsh way, but I didn't mean to. It was just a foolish thing for her to say. What on earth was I going to be doing out there, when Josiah was in here?

"All right," Lydia whispered softly.

It was the third day that Josiah was just lying there. I played checkers with him, pretend-like, and told him stories about Celeste. "The last I heard of her," I said, "She was in New Orleans, eating alligator. And loving it."

Ma and Caleb showed up. We ate some dinner that Ma brought us, and then she took me home. Caleb was going to stay with Lydia and help her keep watch.

In the deep of night, I woke. Pa's face was right near mine. He said, "Caleb just sent someone. Josiah's woken up. He wants to see you."

I sat up so fast, the room wobbled. I didn't change out of my nightgown—just put on my boots and my coat. I was soon riding Dakota, my arms tight around Pa's waist. God bless my Pa—for he did not take the slow, long route into town. We ran Dakota through the small woods, along the river, galloping hard.

Stairs two at a time—door opening—the lamplight making a small circle at the top of the bed. Lydia moved aside, and there he was.

"Josiah." I thought I was going to rush forward, but my knees got weak.

He nodded at me. The smile he gave was not his normal, kindly grin that didn't quite reach his eyes. The smile started in his eyes, and spread slowly, all across the room, to me.

Next day, around noon, Josiah and I were playing checkers in a slow way. Lydia, Caleb, Ma, Pa, and Jake were all in the room, talking their grown-up talk.

"I can't believe he didn't come!" Lydia said.

"Who?" I interrupted. All the adults looked at me. Lydia started to shake her head.

"Your pa?" I asked.

Lydia nodded.

"But he did. He was here."

"What?" they all asked.

I nodded. "Not for long. He didn't say anything. But—but you could tell. He was here."

Lydia looked at Josiah. Something passed between them.

That afternoon, all the adults were gone. Ma, Pa, and Jake went back to the ranch. Caleb and Lydia went to get us some ice cream.

I was sitting on Josiah's bed, cross-legged down near his feet. It was time to be honest.

"Josiah," I said. "I talked to Dr. Lowell yesterday. The book. It's not going to make enough money to pay for your own place."

Josiah blinked. "I didn't think it would—"

"I know *you* didn't. But *I* did. I was hoping it would be your way out. And now, even though Dr. Lowell's publishing it, it's not going to be enough. BLAST!" I put my anger into the word. "How can I help you, if our book pays piddly?" I looked down at my hands.

"Clara."

I looked up.

"The book *did* get me out."

"What?"

"Think about it. It did get me out. Every day. A reason to go to the river. To walk around town. Visit Lenwood Farm. Mrs. Foster's. The Heron's."

"But—" I began.

"Stop. I don't think—I don't think you know what it was like before we met on the river. Before and after that, before and after meeting you, and going to the circus, and starting the book. You just don't know."

I didn't know what to say.

He said, "You've never asked, about those letters that got lost in the river when I went nuts—"

"You didn't go nuts—"

"Anyway, you've never asked about those. About what we were going to do."

"I worried about it."

"Clara, we lost the originals. But I had made copies."

"What?"

Josiah looked right at me. "I copied them out so I could read them at home. When I couldn't be out with you." He paused. "See, Clara?"

I nodded slowly. "I think I do." But I had to ask another question. "So what are you two going to do?"

"Lydia and I were talking. We won't go home. Lydia's talking to the hotel clerk here. They might lend us a room, if Lydia works here steady. I'll get a job too. It will be tight. But—we are not going back."

I breathed out slowly. Living in this hotel sounded pretty crummy, but it was so much better than before that my heart was glad. We could fix the room up real nice, too. I could give him my quilt, and that could well lighten a dark room.

The River Boy

And lighten a dark room we did. Later that week, Caleb and Jake and I helped Lydia put together their new home, which was two rooms in the attic of the inn.

When we arrived, Jake shook Lydia's hands and gave a smile. I think Jake was pretty heroic helping us out, so I made sure to be extra nice to him.

We carried up a cute pot-bellied stove and the colorful braided rugs that Ma got out of our attic and even a bookcase that Pa no longer needed. I brought my quilt—consider it on loan, I said—and plenty of sweet-clover sachets.

One of the rooms we turned into a sitting room. Before the stove, we put two old comfy chairs from Mrs. Foster and the bookcase between the windows. Under the low-angled eaves, we snuggled a small table and chair set that the inn owner was lending to Lydia. Lydia had made soft green gingham curtains the night before and pinned them back with a white ribbon. We put nails in the wall and hung their two pots and pan.

As we finished up, I ran down and grabbed a spray of wild, late-summer flowers. From home I had brought an old cream-colored pitcher just for this purpose. I arranged the flowers in the pitcher and set it on the table. It was a flame of color in the attic corner.

I had never seen such a cozy, sweet place. With all my exclaiming, Caleb warned Lydia that she might have a frequent guest. I jostled back that she was sure to have two.

Then, Josiah came up the stairs, leaning against Caleb, walking slowly. His head was bandaged, which made him look kind of interesting, like an old Civil War hero.

When he stepped into the sitting room, I will never forget the look that passed between him and Lydia.

At the end of the day, Jake left for home and Lydia and Caleb went to the grocer's. Josiah and I decided to unpack his trunk. It was high time to put his beautiful collection of books on the empty, waiting bookshelves.

I opened the lid of the trunk—and exhaled slowly in wonder. The inside of the lid had changed since last I saw it. So many more objects were tacked on, arranged with care. I looked carefully at the new collection.

They were artifacts from our summer together—the postcard I had given Josiah of Old Faithful, a spray of dried fireweed, his ticket from Bradley and Murray circus, a paper napkin from Miss Tilly's ice cream parlor, a small fishhook from the hooks that Heron had given us, and of course—cut from a newspaper—our ad.

There was also a folded piece of paper. I looked at Josiah and he nodded. I carefully lifted it my way and unfolded it.

It was my handwriting.

> Sometimes I used to get a kind of hollow feeling before my friend came along. And then when we became friends, the hollowness wasn't near as deep. The thing is, my friend brought all my collections (I have a few) alive.

It was my letter, that I had written for our book.

At the far end of that week, we were at my house, playing checkers before a small fire burning in the hearth. Josiah's head still was bandaged.

It was mid-afternoon. That morning, Lucy, Meredith, Peter, and Jackson had been over. Josiah can't run around too much yet, but the six of us made plans for some late-summer camping a couple weeks later. There was a small island in a river on Boar's Hill that looked just perfect for a campsite. There would be trout to catch and cook and awnings to make with fallen pine branches. Peter kept asking to make sure I would bring enough gingersnaps.

Josiah and I were just setting up our second game of checkers when the front door opened. Caleb and Lydia and Mr. Jim Fry himself walked into our house. Caleb called us all over to where Josiah and I were.

I was nervous to meet Mr. Fry again. I stood up as my parents and Jake introduced themselves.

"Pa," Josiah said. Mr. Fry looked down at him. "This here is Clara, my best friend. She's the one helping me write that book."

I looked up at Mr. Fry. To tell you the truth, I didn't know how I was going to be polite.

He bent down slightly and held out his hand. His eyes were that light brown, just like my friend's eyes. There was no meanness in his face.

"Hello, Miss Clara," he said. I think he was shy.

"Hello, sir," I answered, shaking his hand.

Later that night, Josiah and I walked to the river. We had to walk slowly, of course, but along the way we collected sticks, kindle, and fallen tree limbs. "Here's a doozy!" I cried out, spotting a big, thick log. It looked like the remains of a strong oak branch. I picked it up and dragged it behind me. "This will burn for hours."

"How about here?" Josiah said, choosing a spot on the riverbank that jutted out from the woods. A tall pine tree stood there, its needles leaning over the moving water. At this hour the river was dark, but glints in the current caught the setting sun.

We built a dandy bonfire, logs leaning on each other like a teepee, kindle and brush within. The fire started slow, but it was soon blazing up to the darkened sky.

Josiah threw on a handful of leaves. Sparks flew up. There were big and small, quick and long-lasting, orange and yellow sparks. We lay down, faces to the sky. The night was getting colder.

"Autumn will be here soon," I said. "After a summer to remember." I threw another handful of leaves on the fire. The flames hissed and crackled.

"Best summer ever," Josiah said, rolling onto his tummy, looking at the fire. Then he looked at me. "I can finally tell Dr. Lowell the name of our book," he said. "That is, if you like it."

"What'd you come up with?"

"Look for It Everywhere: Some Letters about Love."

"Josiah," I said softly. "That's beautiful." Then I added, "Your mother would be really proud of you."

"She'd be proud of *us*," Josiah said.

After a couple hours, the fire died out. The night had come to an end. We walked back home together, talking about our book, and what it would be like when it was published, for everyone to see.

This is not near the end of our story, but just the end of a part of one, a story within and alongside many other stories, Caleb's and Lydia's and the Heron's and Lilac's and Miss Tilly's and Dr. Lowell's and even Sophie's. Somehow they all run together like my river does.

Just how the River Boy said they would.

CPSIA information can be obtained
at www.ICGtesting.com
Printed in the USA
FSOW01n0631170616
21645FS

9 780997 640915